RAWHIDE RANSOM

Cole was a good sheriff, maybe a mite too lenient at times, but when the chips were down, the town of Barberry fully appreciated his prowess with guns and fists. But they didn't know there was a tragedy in his past that would affect his actions — until a local boy was kidnapped while Cole was supposed to be guarding him. And the only one who could deliver the ransom was Cole himself.

TYLER HATCH

RAWHIDE RANSOM

Complete and Unabridged

LINFORD
Leicester

First published in Great Britain in 2009 by
Robert Hale Limited.
London

First Linford Edition
published 2010
by arrangement with
Robert Hale Limited.
London

British Library CIP Data

Hatch, Tyler.
    Rawhide ransom.- -(Linford western library)
1. Western stories.
2. Large type books.
I. Title II. Series
823.9'2–dc22

ISBN 978–1–44480–053–1

Published by
F. A. Thorpe (Publishing)
Anstey, Leicestershire

Set by Words & Graphics Ltd.
Anstey, Leicestershire
Printed and bound in Great Britain by
T. J. International Ltd., Padstow, Cornwall

This book is printed on acid-free paper

1

Gunsmoke

As the gunsmoke began to clear it revealed the three dead men sprawled in the dirt of Front Street, thin ribbons of blood trickling into the slush of the gutter.

Adam Cole still remained in the half-crouch he had assumed when the gunfight had become inevitable.

'Damn fools. They could still be alive. Jailbait, but breathing.'

No one was close enough to hear his muttered remark. He commenced to reload his Colt. The townsfolk began to appear from their hurried choices of cover when the bullets started to fly; they had huddled in doorways, behind awning posts and rainwater butts, under parked buckboards, some even lying prone in the street itself, having dropped there hurriedly at the first gunshot.

Dusting down their clothes, all of them stared at the lean sheriff as if they had never seen him before.

In a way they hadn't; this man who had cut down three violent bank robbers in their tracks barely resembled the quiet-spoken, non-violent lawman the town council had hired a couple of months ago. He had been popular because he had good manners: raised, or at least touched, his hat to the ladies in passing on the street, settled many an argument by quiet counselling, or just once or twice with his fists. But those times had been few and far between, though once he took on three drunken trail rowdies passing through and ready to hooraw the town. They tried to blind-side him but all three needed attention from Doc Partridge before quitting town, with Cole riding shotgun out as far as the county line.

Folk had wondered about his gun: a used-looking Colt in oiled leather. No one had seen him even brush his hand against the butt and a few worriedly — and quietly — remarked that they wondered how he would react if he *had* to use it.

Now they knew.

The men he had taken on and who now lay dead in the town's main street had been seasoned outlaws, ready and willing to shoot their way out of trouble. They had been led by Louisiana Dann, notorious for his gunplay and violence.

They came running out of the bank, clutching their booty — and stopped dead when they found the lone figure of the sheriff standing there, casually hipshot, hands hanging down at his sides.

'Stop right there, boys, and you'll see sunrise tomorrow.'

Startled, they had looked around for this lone lawman's back-up — he surely would have five or six deputies planted somewhere . . . ?

There was no sign of even *one*.

3

Good enough for Dann. Playing to the staring, nervous townsfolk, he spoke to Cole: 'You're the one ain't gonna see the sunrise!'

People scattered before all the words were spoken and the guns came up blazing.

There was a brief volley of scattered shots and, later, several witnesses maintained that Cole only fired three times — and Louisiana Dann and his pards lay dead in the dust, the stolen moneybags crumpled under their bodies.

And now the dissipating gunsmoke revealed the whole scene and fast-talking townsfolk crowded around.

'He got all three!'

'Never seen him draw!'

'They had him surrounded — the poor bastards!'

'They never stood a chance!'

Cole was jostled, patted on the back, several men insisted on shaking his hand.

'Someone get a door and take 'em down to the undertaker's.' Cole spoke tersely, obviously uncomfortable with all this attention. 'And get that money back in the bank! Every damn cent!'

'I'm taking care of that, Cole. My clerks will see it's all collected.'

Linus Charlton, the town banker, looked sallow, face drawn, although his figure was corpulent enough and normally his face had a florid, pudden-look. He was trying to light a long thin cigar, his hands shaking, the match flame burning his fingers. Cole snapped a vesta on his thumbnail and held it for Charlton.

'Easy, banker. It's all over. Anyone hurt inside?'

'Uh — two clerks, I think. Yes, Ernie Hall and Benton Ness. One female clerk fainted.'

'They need a doctor?'

'Ernie will. They split his scalp and knocked him cold.' Just then Doctor Partridge appeared, hurrying up with satchel in hand, and the banker directed him inside. Then he looked back at Cole; the cigar seemed to have calmed him some but he had an almost angry look on his face. 'By God, I — we never expected to see anything like this, Cole!'

'What you hired me for.'

'Yes — and thank God we did hire you. Just three shots and that gang is ready for Boot Hill! How come you never told us how good you were when the committee interviewed you?'

'They asked if I was fast with a gun and I said I'd been fast enough so far.' His deep voice held hardly any interest. He jerked his head at Charlton and walked to the law office on the opposite side of the street, the crowd opening out to let him pass.

He was seated at his desk, rolling a cigarette when the banker puffed in, half-smoked cigar down at his side. He dropped into a chair.

'I think this calls for a drink.'

The sheriff fired up and swung the chair around, bending to open a drawer in the desk. He set a whiskey bottle and two shot glasses on the paper-cluttered top and poured two drinks, filling each glass to the brim.

The banker spilled a lot of his before tossing it down. Cole sipped about half, savouring the taste.

'You seem a bit . . . put out, Cole. Look, don't worry about Dann and his friends. They were scum. They'd killed a lot of people over the years. They're better off dead.'

'Would seem that way.'

Charlton frowned. 'This . . . bother you? Hell, man, your reputation will sky-rocket! You'll be known all over the county, maybe the whole damn state, as the fastest gun ever to come — ' He stopped abruptly at the look on Cole's face. 'Is that what's bothering you? Word'll get out about your gunspeed and . . . '

Cole savagely crushed out his barely smoked cigarette in the old coffee-can lid, grey-blue eyes pinched down and cold.

'That's exactly what bothers me, banker! Every goddamn rowdie from here to hell — and back — will show up and want to try my speed!'

'Well, I doubt any of 'em'll be faster than you! Why, the way you got that Colt out ... My God! This has happened to you before, hasn't it?' Cole stared bleakly. 'But I don't recall the name ...'

'Different from the one I'm using now. You wouldn't know it if you heard it.' The sheriff shook his head sharply. 'Damn! I should've known better, should never've taken this job. But I was broke and you offered good pay and — and this is a *quiet* town! Out of the way of the cattle trails, stage-run once a week, a few drunks on Saturday night, no wild-whooping trail hands wanting to lift the roof!' He tightened his lips. 'Then this ... *situation* arises and there was only one way to settle it!'

'And you sure did that!'

Cole slammed his hand down flatly on the top of the desk, the concussion overturning the empty shot glasses and spilling a few papers to the floor, where they lay ignored.

The banker looked uneasy. 'Er — Cole, I sure as hell hope this isn't going to . . . influence you, whether you stay on or not! I know you were on a three-month trial, but, man, we can't afford to lose you! It might be once in a blue moon when something like today happens, but, by God, when it does, you're the kind of man we want to see behind that badge! Please — and I know I speak for the whole town when I say this — *please* don't even think of quitting! I believe I have enough authority with the selection committee to promise to lift your wage, or maybe present you with a cash token of the town's appreciation. Would you consider those things?'

Cole didn't answer right away. 'Money's not my main interest. I've earned enough for my present needs. It could take me a long way from here.'

The banker was alarmed. 'Oh, now, listen, Cole! Don't make any rash decisions! You go back to your hotel room and relax, think about things.' He lowered his voice. 'There's one real nice young woman down the trail at Banjo Springs. No trouble to send for her. Name of Willow.' He winked and half-smiled. 'And that's appropriate! She clings like a willow but I've never heard her weep yet. Sometimes moan, though, and — '

'Go fix your bank, Linus,' Cole interrupted. 'I don't need any female diversions, or the other kind that comes out of a bottle. I'll think about things and let you know come morning.'

It was flat and final and the banker stood slowly, nodding jerkily.

'All right. But I hope you make the right decision, Cole! It could be a lot more serious than you think.'

The sheriff frowned slightly. Did he imagine it or was there a hint of threat in the banker's words . . . ?

'You like to explain that?'

Linus Charlton waved a hand, a little thrown off his stride now as those chilly eyes bored into him. 'I mean, the effect

10

it's going to have on the town if you decide to move on. It doesn't bear thinking about.'

Cole held the man's gaze a moment longer and said heavily, 'Mebbe I'm tired of moving on, Linus. Hell, no 'mebbe' about it! I've done a lot of it and I really thought I'd found a place here where I could live quietly. You've no idea how disappointed I feel right now.'

The banker's face softened. 'You sure never hesitated to tackle those robbers!'

'I took your money,' was Cole's only comment.

The banker suddenly held out one of his pinkish, uncalloused hands. Cole was surprised but gripped it briefly.

'Stay, Cole. Stay with us. There'll be more money whatever happens, and if there's something else you want as part of the deal — well, you just speak up. And if we can get it for you, it's yours.'

Adam Cole watched him cross the street through the dusty window. There was still a crowd outside the bank, studying the ground where the robbers had fallen.

You can't give me what I want, Banker. No one can.

2

Troubles

There was a kind of delegation and it immediately made Cole edgy. He saw them coming through the law office window, a bunch of the town's businessmen — all members of the select committee — heading his way.

He swore and put away the whiskey bottle; he didn't aim to offer his good booze to this lot. By then they were coming in the door, led by the smiling banker.

'As promised, Cole,' Charlton said, adding a belly laugh for no good reason the sheriff could see. The banker gestured to a man in a frayed frock-coat and a white shirt spotted with food droppings. This was Miles Burnside, the town's only lawyer, still a bachelor and heading fast for sixty years old come December.

He had a small leather valise and opened it, taking out a long manila envelope. Cole saw that his name had been written on it in Burnside's famous Olde English style lettering. The lawyer cleared his throat and held out the envelope.

'On behalf of the good citizens of Barberry, all seven hundred and forty-three — '

'Forty-four, Counsellor,' interrupted Griff Cavanaugh who ran the general store. 'Mrs Grandison whelped another daughter just before breakfast. Doc Partridge sent for a bunch of clean towels, and luckily I'd just gotten in a shipment from — '

Burnside frowned. 'I stand corrected then. Well, adding Mrs Grandison's as yet unnamed daughter to the population, we are happy to present you with this token of our appreciation for saving our money, which was being stolen by the now deceased, Louisiana Dann gang.'

There was a county cheque inside the envelope made out to Adam Cole for the sum of $2,000. His eyes widened a little as he read and Banker Charlton said quickly.

'We trust it will be sufficient for your wants, Cole — but not enough to take you away from our town.'

Cole looked up amd smiled thinly. 'Gents, I do believe I'm being bribed — and that's agin the law.'

The delegation's faces straightened and they all looked at Counsellor Burnside.

He cleared his throat. 'It would only be against the law if you were our duly elected sheriff, Cole. As you are still on probation, as it were, you may accept our offering with a clear conscience — and right after, we can declare you Barberry's official new sheriff, with increased salary. Amount to be determined by negotiation, plus privileges.'

Cole's expression didn't change as he studied the cheque. Then he looked up, smiling all the way this time.

'I thank you gents. I just happen to have a newly polished sheriff's star in my top drawer.'

They laughed as he brought out the badge. The tip of one arm of the star was slightly bent from the accident that had killed the previous sheriff. Emerson, the undertaker and church deacon, said in his usual sin-killing voice, the loudest and most resonant in town,

'I b'lieve we might've saved some money, gentlemen! Seems to me this probationary lawman was plannin' to stay on as sheriff all along.'

That started more laughter and Cole relented. He brought out his whiskey bottle but was short of glasses.

'Fill the ones you've got,' suggested Griff Cavanaugh, 'and pass the bottle round. We ain't too proud to drink our whiskey direct.'

There was unanimous agreement and Mannering, who ran the town's only saloon, went away and came back with six extra glasses and two more bottles of whiskey.

It was just as well no one broke the law in town that afternoon or evening — and part of the night . . .

When they at last decided to leave — two wives had arrived and had stood on the law office porch, berating their now very merry husbands, breaking up the revelry — only Banker Charlton remained. Cole sat down again in his chair, wiped his sweating face and loosened his trouser belt.

'That was . . . pleasant, Linus. Kind of thing I've been looking for. Guess I have you to thank you for it, the money and so on — '

'Not at all. Thank yourself for stopping the robbery. They'd almost cleared out the safe. A *lot* of money would have been missing and a lot of folk would have suffered because of it.'

Cole shrugged. 'Well, the only thing I can add is that I'll give the job a try for a couple of months and — '

Charlton sobered. 'We intend for you to stay in the job a lot longer than that, Cole!'

The sheriff, now wearing the damaged star on his shirt, held up a hand. 'Told you I was looking for somewhere I could settle in peace and quiet, Linus. Reckon there's a good chance of me finding it here. Like you say, that robbery attempt by Dann was unusual, but if it brings in a lot of fellers wanting to try my gun speed . . . ' He shook his head briefly, 'I'll just have to move on.'

'Well, I'll pass this along to the committee, Cole, but it's not what we expected.'

'If you want the cheque back, that's OK. Like Burnside said, I had decided to stay on, but only for a spell, a trial period.'

'Keep the money. Our appreciation of what you did isn't in any way lessened, but we would like to see you as our *permanent* sheriff.'

'Let's see how things work out, Linus.' He wiped a hand across his face. 'Whew! I like the odd snort but I'm glad we don't have a session like this every night.'

Banker Charlton smiled. He, too, was feeling the effects of the whiskey. He glanced at his gold pocket watch and heaved to his feet.

'I sure as hell better be going. Bess will be blowing steam out of her ears by now. My dinner will be either burned or cold — or maybe the dog got lucky!'

They laughed and Cole closed the door behind him, turned the key in the lock and leaned against the paint-peeling wood. His tired eyes travelled slowly around the lamp-lit office.

'Well, you could've said 'no, thanks'. Now you're stuck here for at least a couple of months. He glanced at the tattered calendar on the wall. His gaze went immediately to July 7 — a Friday, just under four weeks away. He felt his belly knot. Damn fool! You should've made that a one-month trial, not two. Now you'll be here when it comes around — the first time in five years you haven't passed that day — and *night* — alone, in some isolated place with just the stars and the wilderness and no one to see, or hear, but you, your horse and God — if he's anywhere around!'

He glanced at the whiskey bottle on the desk. There was a good inch remaining in the bottom.

He snatched it up and drained it, then groped his way to his chair, slumped into it and drifted away into a disturbed sleep.

★ ★ ★

Bess Charlton was Linus's second wife. As well as a deal of property and cash left by her deceased first husband, she had brought to the marriage, Donny, her eight-year-old son. As far as Linus was concerned the kid was the biggest pain in the butt he had experienced since an acute attack of the piles.

Probably Donny was no better or worse than the average eight-year-old, but there was instant hostility between him and Banker Charlton. Donny didn't even like the name and tried to keep his original one: Curtis.

Bess wouldn't hear of it. 'I'm marrying Linus Charlton, Donny, and that's the name I will take. You are my flesh and blood, so you will now become Donny Charlton. I'll have no argument! That's it!'

Bess was a woman used to having her own way and one time, in a fit of pique, Donny had told her this, adding that she had been 'spoiled' by Lawrence Curtis. It was the last time Donny sassed his mother about that.

But he turned his juvenile anger and frustration towards Charlton, who was not much good with children anyway.

'You're not my father!' Donny often used this statement of truth when Charlton hardened his voice and tried to exert authority over the boy for one reason or another. 'I don't like you!'

'Mutual, my dear stepson, I assure you. It's *mutual*!' He looked around swiftly, lowered his voice, his tone not changing. 'And you keep up this insolence and you'll be eating like a horse for a week — *standing up!*'

Donny curled a lip, showing his small white teeth. 'You're not funny! Except for the way you look! Like a ball with a turnip on top!'

Linus almost ruptured himself in exerting the force he put behind the kick he aimed at the darting boy. He missed, of course, and so the effort strained his groin even more. Gasping, clutching his side low down, he managed a curse.

'I'll fix your wagon . . . one of these days, kid! You can count on it!'

Donny pressed a thumb to his upturned, freckled nose and waved all four fingers in the current ultimate insulting gesture at the small Barberry school.

Bess was aware that the relations between her new husband and her eight-year-old were dismal and after a while she gave up trying to improve them. Sometimes — most times — she took the boy's part anyway and this made her own relations with Linus less than sweet and wonderful.

But they survived and they lived very well, probably better than anyone else in Barberry. This was in part due to Linus's good salary from the Frontier First National Bank. He was paid well to manage this out-of-the-way branch in a small town like Barberry. The lifestyle was occasionally given a lift by Bess's own contribution from money left to her by her dead husband. *Only occasionally*.

By the accepted and unwritten law of the day, her bank balance and property holdings were supposed to be accessible to Linus at any time. But when he first made her aware of this, she placed a hand on one of her ample hips, narrowed those icy-blue eyes and shook her blond head.

'No, Linus. Curtis earned this money and invested wisely. It has nothing to do with you. It was all for the benefit of Donny and myself. I believe you will find me generous on occasion, but it will be at my option.' Then she smiled that devilish smile that got him all heated and short of breath. 'And I haven't heard any complaints from you when I have felt generous with my . . . favours in the past.' She laughed lightly at the flushed look on his face, knew why he was squirming.

He swallowed, nodded, drew out a kerchief and mopped his heated face swiftly. 'As you will, my dear. After all, it's your money . . . '

But he would love to get his hands on some of it! Deuce Mannering ran such marvellous card games in the rear of his saloon, late at night . . . If he could only match some of the bets made by these visiting ranch owners from the neighbouring county whom he invited to the game!

Cards and dice had always thrilled him; once he lost an appointment in a Missouri bank because of his liking for gambling. 'Not appropriate for a bank manager, Mr Charlton. Sorry.'

Still, lately he had done all right with a little manipulation, which no one had detected or even known about, let alone Bess.

But there was some pressure on him by Mannering, who actually worked for the big saloon owners in Banjo Springs. They called their gaming rooms (legal in Banjo County) casinos — a foreign word, but with a wonderful sound to it, like cards slithering and dice rattling.

★ ★ ★

The first fast gun arrived in town on the second stage after the thwarted bank robbery. A little under two weeks.

He didn't look very different from the cowboys and drifters who passed through the town. He wore range clothes that had seen better days, a leather vest with a tobacco-sack tag dangling from the left upper pocket, a single gunbelt and holstered Colt, scuffed riding boots, tarnished spurs.

He swung a warbag casually over his shoulder and stopped a depot clerk, easing back his curlbrim hat from his face.

'Friend, can you point me in the direction of the law office?'

'Why, sure. Turn left at the gate and end of the lane is Front Street. Left again and it's about halfway along.' The clerk, young and impressionable, added, 'Er . . . You heard about our Sheriff Cole? An' how he stopped the Louisiana Dann gang dead when they tried to rob our bank?' He winked. 'An' I mean *stopped 'em dead*!'

The cowboy nodded slightly, smiled; he had a pleasant enough face, hard-jawed, but maybe the eyes had a mean look to them. 'B'lieve I did hear somethin'. Fluke, weren't it?'

'Fluke? Like hell! If you'd seen Cole move — well, you wouldn't've. No one seen him draw. Just his gun was suddenly there in his hand, blazin', and them three robbers were down in the dust. Not even kickin' they died so fast.'

The cowboy's smile had disappeared

now. 'No one's that fast! Not even Hickok.'

'I dunno 'bout that. Mr Hickcok ain't never been to this town, but I sure wouldn't care to go up agin Sheriff Cole — ' He stopped suddenly, looked sharply at the man, noting now that the base of the holster, worn quite low on the thigh, was tied down with a rawhide thong. The leather had been cut away around the trigger guard to allow swifter access for the finger and . . . The clerk swallowed. 'I — I best get on with my work, mister. Just do what I said and you'll find the law office. All right?'

'Yeah, sure. Thanks, friend.'

He flipped a quarter and the clerk deftly caught it. He watched the man stroll up the lane, the warbag slung over his shoulder — his *left* shoulder he now noticed, keeping his gun arm swinging free.

He hurried back into the depot, calling to one of the drivers who was filling out his usual papers:

'Zeke! I . . . I think there's gonna be another shootin'.'

★ ★ ★

Cole was seated at his desk, writing up some reports for the town council when a shadow darkened his doorway. The dusty cowboy stood there, framed by the bright sunlight from the street, no more than a blurred outline to the sheriff.

Recognizing the ploy, Cole was immediately alert and laid down his pen. 'Come on in.'

'I'll do my talkin' from here.'

Cole nodded and thrust slowly to his feet. 'Then I better come across and get a look at you.'

As he stepped around the desk and approached the doorway the man smiled crookedly. 'They call me Flash Jack Cotton.'

Cole stopped, leaning one hand on the edge of the door. He nodded. 'Expected you earlier.'

28

Cotton blinked. 'You don't know me!'

'And don't want to. But you're no different from any other two-bit *pistolero* who figures he's the fastest gun alive and aims to prove it by outdrawing me.'

Cotton smiled again. 'You're lookin' right at him, Cole. Make it good, 'cause I'm gonna be the last thing you ever see.'

'Getting right down to it, huh?' Cole sighed. 'Well, guess that's the best way. OK. Let's get it done.'

Then he slammed the door closed and heard the muffled cry of agony through the heavy woodwork and the clatter as Cotton was smashed back against the porch rail. It gave way and the cowboy sprawled on his back in the street, warbag flying into the slush of the gutter.

By that time Cole was standing on the landing, looking down at the man who now had a bloody face and was struggling to stand. Cole held up a hand — his left. 'Be wise to stay put, friend. Unless you're gonna make a run for the depot. You'll just about make the stage turn-around.'

Flash Jack Cotton had other ideas, as Cole knew he would; the man hadn't come all this way to be knocked down by a swinging door. He thrust to his feet, stooped over and half-turned towards Cole as if making an effort to push upright. Instead, his Colt left leather with a deadly whisper and flame spurted from the barrel as he spun, fully facing Cole now.

Not for long. Cole's lead took him in the crook of his gun arm and he screamed as he floundered back, his arm jerking violently, bone splinters tearing through the bloody flesh. Cotton's smoking Colt spun from his fingers, which could no longer hold its weight.

And never would again.

A crowd gathered in moments, folk running up from all directions. Cole picked out the sweating stage clerk.

'Billy, have someone help you get him to Doc Partridge. This fool's got money jangling in his pocket so he can pay for whatever attention Doc gives him. Put the rest towards a stage ticket back to Banjo Springs — or as far as it'll take him.' He swung his bleak gaze to the writhing, sobbing would-be gunfighter. 'He won't be coming back to this town.'

3

Ultimatums

Ten days later the second challenger arrived, coming in from the north.

He rode a dust-spattered paint with a sidekick forking a shaggy roan alongside. The one who turned out to be the challenger was a small man, no more than five feet four or five. He wore two guns on a *buscadero* rig with plenty of fancy carving in the leatherwork. *Spanish*, most folk said, recognizing the style as coming from below the Border.

Someone with better eyes than the others and more knowledge of guns pointed out that the Colts' handles had been shaved down to allow a better fit in the man's small hands.

The men rode straight past the law office, not even glancing in its direction, and dismounted outside Mannering's Delta saloon.

Inside they ordered whiskey and the taller one pushed a coin towards the barkeep from the change pile.

'Have one yourself.'

'Thanks, *amigo*, but boss don't allow it. You boys from up north?'

'What makes you say that?' demanded the small man, sounding irritated.

'That yaller dust all over you. Has to be from the Canary Desert.'

'Everyone a smart-ass in this town or just you?' the aggressive man cracked. The barkeep straightened and moved away down the counter. The small man slapped a hand down hard on the scarred woodwork. 'Hey, you! I asked you a question!'

The tall man placed a hand on the other's arm. 'Easy, Frankie, we don't need trouble here.'

'Why not? It'll bring Cole, won't it?'

'That ain't how we planned it!'

'Trouble with you, Biff, you're bigger'n me but your brain's smaller.

You can't adapt to a change in plans.' And as he spoke he whipped up one of his guns, the left one, and shot out the bar mirror. Glass and bottles leapt in a wild cascade, cutting the cringing barkeep. The man held a grey bar towel to his bleeding face.

'The hell you doin'?'

'Gettin' your attention — or your sheriff's. If he ain't too busy, or somethin', to come see what's happenin'.'

Biff groaned, seeing it was way too late to stop his smaller pard now.

'You might be sorry if Cole does come!'

The barkeep yelped and jumped as Frankie fired over the counter, his bullet taking the already bleeding man in the foot. He collapsed, gritting his teeth, stifling a howl of pain.

Mannering, watching from his office doorway, spoke quietly over his shoulder to someone behind him. 'Go get Cole.'

'No need, boss.' A hand came over

Mannering's shoulder, pointing in the direction of the batwings which had just slapped back. Cole entered, gun still in holster, but eyes darting around the smoke-dimmed room, his body tense, his movements catlike and alert.

He soon saw the source of the trouble, and identified it immediately as Frankie bared his teeth, holstering his six-gun.

'Biff, I b'lieve we are now honoured with the presence of Sheriff Adam Cole, self-styled fastest gun alive — the poor bastard!'

'You're Frankie Delgado.'

'Glad you recognize me.' The pigeon chest puffed out some.

'Saw you once in Fort Griffin. You shot a half-drunk buffalo runner, wounded him, made him crawl along the street and howl like a dog, shooting at him all the time. Till you finished him off. Thing is, one of those bullets ricocheted and killed a lady on a hotel balcony, knitting a shawl for the baby she hoped to have in a few weeks.'

Delgado wasn't pleased at the accusation but didn't deny it. 'Main thing was, you seen how fast I am. That buff-runner was really Hi-Spade Hunnicutt, hidin'-out after killin' a man in El Paso. Man he killed was a pard of mine. Hi-Spade deserved to die.'

'The pregnant woman didn't.'

Delgado sobered, then shrugged. 'OK, you wanna make that the excuse to try to take me in,'s OK by me.' He set his short legs firmly and the crowd pressed back — but not too far. Everyone wanted to see this. 'But I ain't goin' with you!'

Biff leaned against the bar after moving along a little way, putting some distance between Frankie Delgado and himself. But just far enough along so that he was slightly to the rear of the sheriff, who hadn't taken his eyes off the small man.

'Guess you're not too confident, Frankie. Having Biff there ready to cover you in case you're not as fast as you figure.'

Delgado looked fit to bust. 'The hell I ain't!'

36

And that was it: no more talk. It was put up or shut up time.

He was damned near as fast as he believed. Frankie's guns seemed to snap into line with his hands braced against his small hips as they blazed.

Cole staggered even as he fired. One shot. It almost took Delgado's head off, snapping it back as if his neck was made of wet cardboard. The impact lifted his small feet from the sawdusted floor, hurling his body against the bar. He was still falling towards the floor when Biff triggered and Cole's second bullet took him through the heart.

And, to the surprise and consternation of the drinkers, their sheriff was down on one knee, head hanging, gun hand on the floor, the arm supporting his weight.

★   ★   ★

A few weeks after the bank robbery attempt, Bess floored Linus with her announcement over dinner:

37

'I'm thinking of taking a trip to the West Coast, Linus. I know you can't get away from the bank at this time of year, so it will be just Donny and me. It's time he met his Uncle Carl.'

Charlton almost choked on the last boiled potato and had to snatch at the water jug to fill his glass, but Donny, with an innocent smile, reached the jug first. He not only pulled it quickly towards him but knocked it over, spilling its contents.

'Gee, Linus,' he refused to call him 'Dad' or 'Father', even 'Pop' — 'I'm sorry. I — I'll go pump some more in a minute and fill the jug. You be OK till I get back? I mean, I wouldn't want you to choke or anything — '

'Donny!' shouted Bess, half-rising, eyes narrowed. 'Get through to the kitchen and pump that water! Hurry, you little devil!' She lunged towards her gagging husband and clapped him between the shoulders as Donny strolled towards the kitchen doorway.

'Move, damn you!' It was the first

time Linus had heard her use a cuss-word and Donny sure looked surprised. He started to run.

After Linus had settled down and was massaging his flabby throat, she made the boy apologize, which Donny did — with the worst possible grace. He was sent to bed without any more supper, but Linus knew she would sneak him a piece of pie or some kind of sweetmeat later.

'So. You've timed your holiday to coincide with the busiest part of the year for my bank! The land sales, reassessment of mortgages, my inspection of outlying farms we have loaned money on — '

'I'm sorry, dear. You know I'm impulsive, and once I get an idea in my head — '

'Oh, yes! I know, all right! But dammit, Bess, I'd love to see San Francisco.' They had great gambling halls there, he had been told, the stakes sky-high: why, some of the richest land-and-cattle owners in the US had gotten their start in the 'Frisco gaming halls.

'Well, it'll be better if we go now, before Donny starts the more serious side of his education. I wouldn't want to interrupt his schooling.'

'Oh, goodness, *no*! That would be unthinkable. How long do you estimate to be away?'

'I haven't given it much thought — a few weeks, I daresay. I might even spend the winter there. Carl says it's much milder and there are no blizzards like the ones that sweep this God-forsaken hole . . . '

'Months! And what the hell am I going to do? Who's going to keep house for me? Make my meals, wash my clothes . . . ?'

Of course, Bess didn't do those things now: they had a live-in cook and maid-of-all-work, and Bess coolly reminded him of that now. 'You'll be well looked after, Linus, dear.'

'Your mind's made up, I see.'

'Yes. It just . . . came to me. All

detailed and everything. I need some decent clothes. I'm sick of mail order and never getting exactly what I expect. Curtis sent me to New York once, and Philadelphia and it was marvellous. I will, naturally, use my own money. You won't be out of pocket.'

'I would not expect to be! Damnit, Bess, Curtis didn't have the responsibility of running a bank!' growled Linus, knowing it was no use throwing one of his tantrums: she was too damn hard for that to work. 'He could afford to pamper you and . . . ' He let the words trail off. What was the use? She was immovable.

But, by God, he would throw a spanner in the works if he could. Just the thought of that smirking little swine enjoying the sights of an exciting town like 'Frisco while he slaved away at all the problems this time of year seemed to magnify . . .

'I'm going for a walk,' he announced abruptly.

'Would you like my company, dear?'

41

Bess asked sweetly. 'It's a balmy might and — '

'My own company is all I can stand right now!'

'Of course, dear. I agree wholeheartedly.'

He grunted as he jammed on his hat and strode angrily out into the night.

He hadn't gone half a block before he stopped dead on the boardwalk.

My God! That sneaky damn Jezebel! Curtis's brother, Carl, was a lawyer and executor of his brother's will. He took care of the estate, advised Bess how she should spend or invest her money. Audited the books . . .

He knew she had received a letter from Carl a couple of weeks ago. Now she had *impulsively* decided to make the long, arduous trip to California, taking Donny with her. That part was OK, but why was she going now and what was she taking with her?

'Oh, blast!' Linus hissed, unaware of the beauty of the star-studded evening and a couple of passers-by wishing him 'Good night'.

He felt sick to his stomach.

He turned and hurried back towards the large house on the hill at the end of Lavender Street.

He had just remembered he had left the keys to the house safe on his bedside table; there were things in there she shouldn't see!

Linus began to run.

4

Independence Day

Cole had set up a chair with footrest on the Front Street balcony of the Star Hotel where he had booked a room after receiving his 'appreciation bonus' from the town committee. Prior to that, he had slept in the small room out back of the law office, even, on one occasion, spent a night in one of the cells, trying out the bunks: no feather bed.

Now he figured he could afford a little luxury so why not enjoy it?

The footrest had been designed by Doc Partridge and consisted of cushions placed in the top part of two crosspieces of wood forming two 'Xs' and connected by slats of timber. It formed a kind of cup and supported Cole's foot and lower leg. And he needed it; Delgado's bullet had creased his left hip and it still hurt enough after a couple of weeks for him to have to use a stick when getting around.

At least there had been no more challengers since Delgado and Biff had taken up residence in the Barberry Boot Hill. He had decided that if any more drifters came in and wanted to test his gun speed, he would pull up stakes. He was reluctant to do that, because he liked Barberry and its folk. It was a town that would have a good future when this part of the country was opened up by more railroads; but he would probably move out before then.

He was a small-town man, always had been. Luckily, Alice had shared his liking for such places and if things had been different . . .

He reined in his thoughts right there. Nothing could change it now so what was the point in thinking about it?

But he knew the present date, July 1, and that meant the time he dreaded was drawing close. Not the Fourth, with its planned celebrations, but the Seventh, which had a different kind of meaning for him.

'How's the leg, Cole?'

He started a little at the enquiring voice, hitched around and saw Banker Charlton coming towards him along the balcony. The man's left hand was heavily bandaged and he held it level across his waist as if to ease its discomfort.

Cole stared at it as he answered slowly, 'Gonna throw away this damn stick in another day, whether I fall flat on my face or not.'

Linus smiled, sat down in a wicker chair and lit one of his cigars, awkwardly, mostly using his right hand and the two unbandaged fingers. He offered the case to Cole, who shook his head and rolled a cigarette.

'What happened to your hand?'

The banker waved his cigar, trying to be casual but there was tension there and an abruptness to his words that made it clear he didn't want to discuss it in detail.

'Tripped on one of Bess's confounded mail-order floor rugs in my office. Put my hands out to save myself and cracked a couple of fingers. Painful but more of a nuisance than anything.' He drew quickly on his cigar and exhaled the smoke, speaking as he did so. 'The committee's arranged for the Miller brothers to be on call if you need them to lend a hand on the Fourth's celebrations. Satisfactory, Cole?'

Cole nodded curtly. 'Hope they won't be needed.'

'We-ell, it *is* Independence Day. Folk might get carried away some. Kids are always a bit of a problem, letting off fireworks with no thought of where they light them or where they might land.'

Cole's face suddenly straightened out. 'If kids are the biggest problem, that'll suit me,' he said curtly. 'With all that home-brewed rotgut being handed round, though, there's going to be a slew of drunks.'

Charlton frowned. 'Well, folk have to let their hair down now and again. Er

— can I ask you a favour? Keep a special eye on young Donny? He's an irritating kid and I confess I don't get along too well with him, but — well, he's Bess's son and I wouldn't want any real harm to come to him.'

'Just a little harm'll be OK, though, eh?'

Linus blinked, sat up straighter. 'I didn't mean it that way! I — Oh! You're joshing me.'

'Trying to. That's how bored I am, Linus, amusing myself with feeble jokes.'

'Once you get back onto your feet and have a few celebratory drinks on the Fourth, you'll perk up. Will you watch out for Donny?'

For a moment the banker thought the sheriff was going to refuse, but he nodded jerkily. 'Sure. But I guess I'll have plenty to do so don't expect me to follow him around and wipe his nose for him.'

'Of course not. He can wipe his own nose, anyway. But he admires you, like all the kids in town, following you around, playing 'Sheriff Cole' with wooden guns and so on. I'll be obliged, Cole.'

'I'll see he doesn't get into any trouble.' Struggling some, Cole got his stick and used it to lever himself out of the chair, putting his left foot down gingerly, transferring the weight a little at a time. 'Ah! Feels better than it did yesterday. Think I'm getting there, Linus.'

He leaned on the stick, looking steadily at the banker's bandaged hand, then lifted his gaze to Linus's face. The man seemed uncomfortable under that stare. 'Haven't had much to do except sit up here and watch the street and passing parade for a few days, Linus.' The hard eyes seemed to bore into Charlton. 'See folk come and go.'

'Uh-huh,' Linus said carefully as Cole paused.

'Day before yesterday I saw a feller come out of your bank. Not by the street door, though he went in that way.

He left by the side door that opens directly from your office.'

Linus looked pale now, his face taut. The smile he forced didn't work, but he didn't speak.

'Big feller with a beard, wide shoulders, cannonball head, dressed well enough but wearing his gun low and tied down. That's what got my interest, so I looked a little more closely. Know the man I'm talking about?'

Linus shook his head, ran a tongue around his lips. He seemed to have forgotten the burning cigar and a long, sagging cylinder of ash dropped down the front of his waistcoat, but he didn't notice.

'He wouldn't've come out of my office. There's a short, narrow passage leads down from our file storage. It connects with the foyer one end, and behind a partition, to that side door at the other.'

'Doesn't sound like a good arrange-ment for keeping your bank secure, not if anyone can use it. But how would the feller I'm talking about know about it? This is the first time *I've* heard of it.'

Linus shrugged. 'It's no real secret, but it's hidden mostly by a couple of large potted plants. He may've just been poking around and noticed it. What're you getting at, anyway, Cole?' He tried to harden his voice but he was not successful.

'I know that man, Linus. He comes from Banjo Springs. He's called 'Quick' Quinlan. Dunno whether it refers to his claim to be half-brother to a bolt of lightning with a gun, or how ready he is to use his fists and boots. He enjoys crippling people.' He watched the tension taking hold of the banker, lowered his gaze to the bandaged hand, adding, 'He's Brack Devlin's trouble-shooter.'

'Devlin? The man who runs the big gambling hall down in the Springs. Calls it a 'casino'?'

'You know who I mean. Devlin's tough. They say he's got connections to a gambling syndicate on the East Coast.'

'I've heard that, too, but . . . I still don't know what you're getting at.'

'Linus, if you're in any kinda trouble, and Quinlan's part of it, you better tell me about it now.'

Charlton snorted, smiling crookedly. 'Trouble? Me? With people like that? What would I be doing dealing with Brack Devlin or — '

'Only way you'll deal with Devlin is through Quinlan — and I saw him leaving your office two days ago. And now you show up with busted fingers. One of Quinlan's little 'demonstrations'? A kind of preview of what could happen?'

'I just told you, that door can be reached by — ' The banker sounded annoyed and Cole broke in rudely.

'Know what you *told* me, Linus. Maybe it's so, maybe not. But Quinlan wouldn't traipse all the way up here to do business with your bank when Devlin already has his own set-up in

Banjo Springs. If he came to see you, it was on behalf of Devlin.'

'Look, you're way off, Cole! I don't know what you're implying, exactly, but I have no dealings with this Quinlan, and certainly not with Brack Devlin! It would be more than my job's worth to get involved with a crook, and a *gambler* at that!'

Cole levelled his gaze at the banker and Linus couldn't hold the stare, dropped his eyes, involuntarily rubbing his bandaged hand lightly. He straightened his shoulders. 'I have to be going, Cole. I'll be obliged if you'll keep an eye on young Donny on the Fourth and — '

'Already said I would. Linus, before you go . . . I consider you a friend and if you have any problems, I'll be glad to help out.' He lifted a hand as the banker started to protest. 'I know Quinlan, and I've seen his work. I spent six months working for Careful Carmody on his freight line. Won't go into details but we made a run to Banjo and through no fault of his own, Carmody ran into trouble with Devlin. Devlin turned Quinlan loose. Carmody's retired now, still uses crutches. Me and the other freighters didn't fare too well, neither. I can give you the full story if you like, but take it from me, Linus, don't tangle with Quinlan. Bring me into it and I'll help you all I can.'

The banker began to bluster, working at it.

'I've had enough of this! Who d'you think you are, accusing me of dealing with the likes of Brack Devlin? I've tried to tell you — '

'Linus! Quinlan's the one to look out for. OK, he comes to see you, has a chat, mebbe over a cigar and whiskey, fairly pleasant . . . ' He glanced pointedly at the injured hand. 'Fairly. But you've been warned now, just a hint of what might come your way. Wait, damnit! Let me finish. Next time won't be anywhere near so pleasant — there'll be a lot more than finger bones being cracked.'

Charlton was breathing hard now, his

face deeply flushed, nostrils flaring, thick chest heaving. There was a lot of fear there but he was trying to cover it with anger.

'Damn you, Cole! Mind your own business! Now, that's all I have to say. Good-day!'

Cole watched him stride away angrily along the veranda, felt sudden aching pain in his hip and sat down again, using both hands to lift his leg back onto the rest.

He hoped he was wrong about Linus, but he knew he wasn't; the banker had somehow run foul of Devlin and his fixer had Linus in his sights.

He had been seriously thinking of moving on after the Seventh, but now . . . He'd already said it: he considerd the banker a friend and a man doesn't walk away from a friend in trouble.

★   ★   ★

The Fourth of July started with a bang — literally. Some farm boys, in for the celebrations, having to bring their wives to town early so they could help cook the goodies for breakfast and other meals, also brought in a good supply of moonshine. And gunpowder, in newspaper-wrapped packages in flour-sack carry bags slung across their chests and shoulders.

It was traditional that the law turned a blind eye to illicit stills at this time of year. In any case, sampling their neighbours' efforts meant passing several different stone jugs of the elixir from hand to hand. By the time a man had sipped all of the various brews, his taste-buds were numbed — and so was much of his brain.

No one was certain afterwards who first suggested they unlimber the Civil War cannon outside the council hall. The idea was to load it and salute The Flag, flapping desultorily at the top of the white-painted mast on the small lawn, with pyramids of cannonballs each side of the gun.

The moonshine was taking effect by

the time a merry group ran the cannon out of its footings and into the small town square, deserted at this time; most of the activities were out at the barbecue pits and the fires of the designated cooking area, or in setting up tables at the old swimming hole.

Stumbling, staggering into one another, each man insisted on pouring some of his very own 'special' mix of gunpowder into the barrel. Their minds were too fuddled to keep count, and just in case there *had* been a short-count, they tossed in a few extra measures. Then they lit the fuse from a burning cigar and ran for cover.

Just as well they did.

The cannon exploded, hurling the breech and a portion of the barrel down a side street and clear over the roof of the double-storeyed Delta saloon. Pieces of shattered iron peppered and clattered against stores and houses; glass tinkled, wood splintered, frightened horses at hitch racks in connecting streets shied and whinnied, dogs ran whining for cover, cats raced, meowing in terror, up tall trees.

Irate citizens swarmed into the smoke-choked square — in Cole's case, *limped* in — but no one was to be seen. Only the shattered cannon and the broken gun-carriage. The flag pole was leaning at a new and potentially dangerous angle, too.

A slurring voice, its owner well hidden somewhere not too far away, bawled, '*Hap-pee Independence Day!*'

And a half-dozen voices cut loose with Rebel yells.

★ ★ ★

That insane, booming blast set the tone for the rest of the day. It would be the noisiest, drunkenest celebration Barberry had ever seen.

There were several fights even before breakfast, but Cole, limping, his leg hurting like hell, let them sort themselves out. Mostly the combatants were too drunk to stand, let alone land damaging punches.

It was noisy, as was to be expected; fireworks were exploding and hissing and arcing all over the large picnic ground near the bend of the river. Smoke drifted in choking clouds, stung eyes, rasped nostrils. But no one seemed to mind. Everyone was here to have a good time — Hell, it was *Independence Day* — only happened once a year didn't it? And a damn good day to celebrate to the full . . .

Cole knew he had to be lenient, turn a blind eye and not harry folk. Food seemed endless, the long wooden trestle-tables sagged under the weight of a hundred different dishes, prepared by the ladies of Barberry. The fiddlers started fiddling and flutes began trilling their sweet notes — not always playing the same tune. Someone produced an empty coal-oil drum, stole a couple of big ladles from the cooking area and wrapped the bowls in dishcloths. In minutes they had a booming bass drum, also throbbing to its own rhythm, the drummer bleary-eyed, lost in a fuzzy world of his own. But eventually, the musicians — or those posing as such — were prevailed upon to play the same tunes. The centre of the wooden platform was cleared and as the toe-tapping notes of *Turkey in the Straw* and *Buffalo Gals* filled the reeking air, the space became crowded with dancers.

There were many stumbles and elaborate, drink-slurred apologies. But when the men realized they were failing to impress their partners, insults were hurled, offence taken swiftly, followed by flying fists.

Most men were already way too drunk to cause injury, but Cole had to move in when a knife was drawn. Limping and gritting his teeth against his pain, he cracked two heads together and dragged the semi-conscious men away to sleep it off under some trees.

Trouble was, every time he went to someone's aid, there was always someone standing by to offer him a drink in appreciation of his efforts.

After a while, refusal not only became boring, but downright dangerous.

'Hey! This ain't panther piss, y' know! I been sweatin' over a hot still for nigh on two weeks, so don't you insult me by refusin' my liquor, Sher'f!'

He escaped a couple of wildly swinging bottles but had consumed a good deal of liquor himself after realizing the raw brew deadened the knifing pain of his wound. Would it do the same for the other pain on the Seventh? He underestimated the powerful effects of the moonshine. It caught up with him suddenly, unexpectedly. Waves of dizziness and queasiness overwhelmed him and he ran staggeringly for the shadows of some trees to rest up a spell. Just a minute or two. *Wait. Where was Donny Charlton?* He hadn't seen the boy for a while; last time was down at the swimming hole with a bunch of his friends. He had sent Josh and Joel Miller down that way to keep an occasional eye on the boy. He had better go and check with them and . . .

Sudden illness ambushed him and Donny Charlton slipped from his mind.

Wiping his mouth, he only now realized that it was quite dark under the trees here, heading towards sundown. Where the hell had the day gone? He leaned against a tree, head swimming. Maybe he'd sit and have a smoke, then go look for the kid and ·. . .

The fist came out of nowhere, drove into his kidney area and slammed him face first into the rough bark of the tree. Lights burst and whirled behind his eyes; he had enough sense to know they weren't Fourth of July firecrackers. Then his legs were kicked out from under him. A boot thudded into his upper chest. A worn heel drove down towards his face. He managed to wrench his head aside just in time, but the heel tore part of his ear. The searing pain sent some sort of sanity through his throbbing brain.

He twisted the foot next time it came swinging in and heaved mightily. Someone yelled, and there were stumbling sounds and curses.

'Kick his goddamn leg wound! *Hurt* the son of a bitch, Quick said. *Do* it!'

That sure didn't sound like just a couple of over-exuberant townsmen! These men were out to hurt him — and badly. He rolled, head spinning, still nauseous, somehow got the tree between himself and his attackers. In the shadows and with his sight blurred from the drink and that initial blow to his kidneys, he could only make out the men as hazy, moving shapes. He twisted violently as a boot drove towards his wounded upper thigh. It missed, but his leg crumpled under him and he fell to one knee. He used his hands to slap away a kick aimed at his face. He up-ended the boot's owner and staggered to his feet, pressing his back into the tree for support. His throbbing leg threatened to collapse again. The second man swung hard. Cole ducked and the man howled as his fist hit the tree full force. While he sucked his popped and cut knuckles, Cole hooked him in the belly, spread a hand over the dimly outlined face and smashed his head against the tree. The attacker started to crumple, moaning.

The other man had regained his balance and came in with a roar, swinging. All the while firecrackers exploded, rockets soared, strident music as well as Rebel yells all drowned out the sounds of the fight.

Cole's leg wouldn't support him any longer. He put out a hand as he started to fall and a knee drove into his face, flinging him back. He struck the tree and sprawled, clawing at the ground, trying to push upright.

But they were onto him now, fists and boots flailing, maiming, grunted words punctuated by the effort behind each blow.

'Mind your — own — goddamn — business in — future!'

'An' — here's somethin' — to help you — re — remember!'

There was an abrupt explosion of light. Then he was tumbling into pitch blackness, racked and jarred with thudding pain . . .

His ears were ringing, his head exploding, filled with noise as if he was standing inside a ringing church bell. And, dimly, through the racket and disorientation, he heard a distant voice:

'Here he is! Behind this tree. Oh, Jesus, he's been in a fight. Aaagh! Smell him!'

'Drunk as a skunk! He's been hittin' the moonshine!'

'Throw some water over him!'

Even through his pain and all the racket, Cole recognized that voice. 'Li — Linus?'

'Yes, damn you, it's me! Where the hell've you been? We've been looking for you for over an hour . . . ' He was shaken roughly. 'Goddamnit, Cole! Don't you pass out on me again! While you've been getting drunk and fighting, young Donny's gone missing! You were s'posed to be watching out for him. *Damnit! Wake up!* D'you hear me? I said *Donny's — gone!*'

5

Lost Boy

Cole was ashamed. He could rationalize a lot of things: pain in the leg wound, rotgut literally forced upon him or there would be hostility and so more trouble to watch out for, and a quiet eagerness on his own part to use the moonshine to deaden other pains that waited just below the horizon, a couple of days away. He could use all these things to tell himself it wasn't his fault: the booze was way too strong, the pain in his leg was intense because he had refused to use a stick at the celebration. But it all came down to one fact: *he got drunk and he was derelict in his duty.*

Donny Charlton was missing and no one knew for just how long. Someone looked around for him late in the afternoon and he just wasn't there, nor anywhere to be found.

All the men, including a distraught and very angry Linus Charlton, were searching the brush and the swimming hole; Donny was a good swimmer, but there were dead trees and other potential snags awaiting the unwary beneath the surface.

Bess was being comforted by the other women and the Independence Day celebrations had now come to an abrupt halt. No fireworks criss-crossed the night sky, no fiddles or Jews' harps filled the balmy air with blood-pounding tunes and much of the uneaten food was spoiled. The coffee pots were continually refilled, though, as weary, unsuccessful searchers staggered in looking for something warm and stimulating.

Cole himself had dunked his head in the swimming hole several times, wanting to change his smelly clothes, but reluctant to leave the scene. He was already the target of many hostile and silently accusing stares.

The Miller boys, Josh and Joel, had done their duty well enough; they had checked on Donny's whereabouts frequently, and there had been nothing untoward. Once his playmate, young Sam Bale, got into trouble in the swimming hole and Donny had helped him ashore. Sam had actually fallen in, his clothes got wet and he became cold. Donny, in a rare gesture of generosity, gave him his jacket to keep him warm.

'Donny wasn't makin' no trouble,' Josh Miller told Cole and the tight-lipped banker. 'Playin' with his friends. Aw, they got a bit cheeky a few times, played pranks, but someone usually stopped things before they got outta hand.'

He looked at his brother for confirmation and Joel nodded. 'They was mostly swimmin', it bein' such a hot day.' He broke off and his gaze was shifty as he glanced at Linus and looked away hurriedly. 'I reckon — sorry, Banker, but seems logical to me — that if we can't find Donny anywheres

around the picnic grounds then . . . '
He jerked his head towards the river.

'No!' snapped Charlton, his well-fed lower jaw trembling. 'No, Donny was a good swimmer! He hasn't drowned!'

'Maybe we better drag the hole, Linus,' Cole said quietly. 'Seems Joel might have something.'

Linus glared at the contrite sheriff. 'I doubt that anyone here will take much notice of your opinions after today, *Sheriff*! I suggest you go home and change those filthy clothes and sleep it off! You aren't much use to anyone right now.'

That hurt Cole but he tried to keep a straight face. 'I can stand my stink a little longer.' He turned to the Millers. 'You boys go organize a dragline . . . '

Charlton grabbed Cole's shoulder and spun him hard enough to make him stagger; pain shot through his leg and he slapped the banker's hand away. It must have hurt because Linus winced and snatched his arm back to his chest, nursing it with his bandaged left hand.

'I'm still sheriff, Linus. Maybe I won't be tomorrow, but for tonight I'm still wearing the badge and I don't have time to waste on stupid arguments. I know I've behaved badly but that won't help us find Donny. Now, you Millers go do what I told you.'

The brothers hurried away and Charlton gave Cole a hard look, mouth tight.

'I'll never forgive you if anything's . . . happened to that boy, Cole!'

The sheriff met his gaze. 'If something has, I'll never forgive myself, Linus.'

* * *

It was a terrible night. Bonfires were lit and the search continued, even though no one considered it ideal conditions for looking.

The men were tired, their weariness increased by the earlier heavy drinking and gluttony. No one really thought they would do a thorough job and an hour or so after midnight, Cole called a halt. He had done as much searching as the others but knew it was hopeless in the dark.

'No, damnit!' gasped the puffing, sweating, staggering banker. 'We are not abandoning this search!'

'Show some sense, Linus,' Cole said wearily. 'Look at these men. Look at yourself. This isn't a search party, it's a bunch of stumblebums. The men are half-asleep, and with hangovers working on them. You can't expect good results — *any* worthwhile results. I think we've pretty well established Donny's not lying on the bottom of the swimming hole, but if he's hurt somewhere, in this brush, and all the shadows, we could walk past him without even knowing he's there.'

'If — if he is hurt,' Linus huffed, 'it's important we find him and — get him medical help as soon as possible.'

They all agreed but backed Cole: no search was going to be successful in the dark. Some of the men were being dragged away by their womenfolk now, others just wandered off, stupid with fatigue.

Linus dropped onto a tree-stump, shoulders slumped, looking down at the ground between his feet.

'I'll give you a hand home, Linus.'

The banker looked up at Cole. 'Go rest your leg! I hope you wake with the god-*damndest* hangover!' He rose, swaying. 'Where — where's Bess?'

'Some of the women took her home earlier . . . '

'How am I going to face her?'

'It was my fault. D'you want me to come in and — '

'I want nothing from you, Cole! Nothing. Except to find that boy, unharmed! Now get your hands off my arm.'

Linus shook the sheriff off and lurched away, mopping his grimy face.

Cole, silent, grim, limped back towards the Star hotel.

★ ★ ★

The next long, long day's search was fruitless, a shambles.

Hangovers killed any real efforts the sick and sorry men tried to make. But they did establish that there were no real tracks; there had been too many kids running about all over the picnic area and particularly around the swimming hole. Cole's questioning, done with squinted eyes and shaking hands so he could barely read the notes he took, produced nothing worthwhile.

Sure, everyone had seen Donny — or at least had seen half a dozen tow-headed boys frolicking and getting up to mischief — and no one had taken any particular notice. There were several strangers in town, but none of them seemed particularly interested in the boys' activities. Most, like the locals, had been looking for free booze and grub.

One man was mentioned, wearing a dark-green shirt, and Cole propped up his ears at that. Some dark-green cloth, obviously torn from a shirt, had been found near where he had fought the men who had jumped him.

The description of the man was vague: average height and build, looked like a cowboy, hard-drinking.

No one could put a name to him.

Later in the day Bess arrived with a few other women, bringing lunch for the searchers. She looked terrible. Normally a handsome woman, she was pale and drawn and her nostrils seemed pinched in, her mouth pursed, giving her a forlorn yet angry look.

She walked right up to Cole, who was leaning on his stick, trying to ignore the ache in his leg, and slapped him once across the face. It turned his head on his shoulders and silence fell around him. He blinked back tears stinging his eyes, looked down at her as her bosom heaved with tremendous emotion.

All he did was nod slowly, admitting he deserved the slap. She turned and lunged away, her hands covering her face, her shoulders shaking with sobs.

Somehow he got through the day but he was still suffering the after-effects of the moonshine when darkness fell and the search was abandoned until tomorrow.

He went to bed without food.

★ ★ ★

There was grey, cheerless light filling his hotel room when Cole slowly swam up through waves of sleep, wincing at the racket of a fist hammering at his door.

'Jesus Christ!' he said, holding his throbbing head. The thunder at the door kept on. 'Who the hell is it? What's up?'

'It's Linus. Open this door at once!'

Cole winced. He couldn't even see clearly. He groped for clothes and sat on the edge of the bed, barely able to move. *That damn rotgut! It was still affecting him!*

What in the hell did they put in that moonshine! His head was exploding, his belly felt as if it had been ripped out, aflame, as if he had swallowed acid. He moaned as he bent forward an inch at a time, trying to find his trouser legs with his feet.

The pounding started on the door again.

'Linus, I swear I'll gutshoot you, you don't get away from that goddamn door!'

He clutched his head again at the sound of his own raised voice. *God, he was so damn tired . . .*

'Can you hurry it up, Cole? This is important.' The banker sounded more reasonable this time, his voice had a tremor in it. 'Very — important.'

'Linus, if I thought you'd done this a'purpose, battered on my door at this ungodly hour just to roust me for . . . whatever the hell it is I did or didn't do. Mind's like a swamp. Can't think clear.'

'It's — it's about Donny!' Charlton's

voice was quieter now, the tremor more noticeable.

Cole frowned, squinting, his eyes almost closed. *Donny*. Any news sounded like it was going to be bad.

'Be but a coupla minutes, Linus,' he called, reeling again from the sound of his own raised voice.

Wearing only trousers, he padded to the door, unlocked it. There were still wall lamps burning in the hotel passage and he held one arm across his eyes as the banker hurried in. The hangover seemed worse today, increased by fatigue.

Cole closed the door and leaned against it, favouring the left leg, bending it slightly and taking most of his weight on the good leg. He squinted at the banker, blinked, trying to clear his vision.

The man looked positively appalling. He was still wearing the clothes Cole had last seen him in at the river. His stubble was showing, and, with the shadows flickering in the room as Cole lit a match and applied it to the table lamp wick, Linus's face was gaunt, despite its normal chubby look. His eyes were sunken and his mouth seemed to pull back tightly against his teeth.

'You look like hell. What's happened?'

Linus Charlton sank down onto the edge of the bed, the bandage on his left hand now grubby and grey, a part of it frayed and dangling. He raised his haunted eyes and his face tightened a little as he looked at the sheriff, who was obviously not in the best of shape himself.

'I — I've called off the search.'

Cole stiffened, felt his belly swirl. 'Ah, no, Linus! Not that! He — he's surely — all right . . . ?'

'How do I know? How the devil do I know anything about him? Whether he's all right, hurt, been knocked about or — '

'Whoa, man! What the hell're you saying? What're you talking about?'

Charlton continued to stare for long moments and Cole thought he had passed into some sort of a trance. Then he stirred and began feeling in the pockets of his dirty, torn coat. He produced a crumpled piece of paper, smoothed it out on one of his fat thighs and stared at it for another long, silent spell. Then, without looking up, he lifted the hand with the paper in it, offering it to Cole.

The sheriff took the paper, moved closer to the lamp. His vision was slowly improving but he had to squint and turn the paper this way and that to read the words crudely printed upon it in pencil:

The kid's OK. He'll stay that way long as you get $20,000 dollars together and keep it handy.

We'll tell you when and how to pay it over. We're not joking banker. Do what we say and you can have the kid back.

Cole read it again, looked up at the banker, sitting on the edge of the bed, shoulders sagging. He wouldn't have been surprised to see a tear running down the grimy, stubbled cheeks.

'Where did this come from, Linus?'

'Pushed under the bank door. I — I went back to change. I keep some spare clothes in my office and didn't want to go home and disturb Bess. She'd taken so long to go to sleep and . . . ' He paused, sighing, shaking his head. 'I was stunned, sat there at my desk, just — staring at it, reading the words over and over, as if they would tell me something . . . '

'You know what it is, of course?'

Charlton nodded slowly, but his voice was hoarse when he answered: 'Of course I know what it is! It's a — a ransom note. They — someone has kidnapped Donny and wants me to pay twenty-thousand dollars to get him back!' He scrubbed a hand down his face. 'Where the hell am I going to get that kind of money?'

Cole frowned. 'Linus, you're president of the local bank — '

The banker's head snapped up. 'Do you think I could touch the bank money! Don't be a damn fool!'

'Surely they'd bend the rules, lend you the money to pay the ransom? You've served them well for years . . . '

'You don't understand these people, Cole. They have stockholders from overseas, England, Scotland, Europe. Those men're thousands of miles away. They're not interested in some Wild West kidnapping! They want *dividends*, not debts!'

Cole scratched his aching head. 'I believe they'd help you out, Linus, but if not . . . there's Bess, isn't there? It's her child and she has a good deal of money if I'm to believe the talk.'

The banker scoffed. 'Talk! Yes, there's been lots of talk — and it's mostly true. Curtis, her first husband, left her pretty well-off. But it's all tied up in property and investments. There is a trust fund for the boy's education and so on and that can't be touched by anyone except his uncle, Carl, who's executor of his brother's will. Bess has access to a small amount for 'expenses' and while it's quite liberal, it's nowhere near the ransom these . . . bastards demand.'

'This Carl . . . can't he be approached? Donny's his nephew. Surely he'll release funds for the ransom?'

'As well he might! But he's a lawyer, Cole — dots every 'i', crosses every 't'. Knows all the legal books backwards. Even if he saw fit to somehow bend his rules, how long d'you think it'd take? With him in San Francisco!'

Cole's leg was throbbing and he sat down on the bed beside the banker.

'I don't see what else you can do, Linus. Approach the bank or this Carl Curtis. If it was me, I'd certainly appeal to the bank.'

'I'd rather they didn't know anything about it.' Linus looked uncomfortable under Cole's quizzical stare. 'I mean — well, you wouldn't understand. When you're responsible for so much money, every day, and there's even a hint of — problems, that could *involve* money . . . ' He shrugged. 'Even though I'm on good terms with head office — well, I don't know, Cole.'

'Then you have to go to Carl, through Bess.'

'I — don't want to bother her with this. She's so — so distraught — '

'Goddamit, Linus! Pull yourself together! You need to raise that money, you have two chances to do it — and you don't want to try either one! You've got to make a decision, man! And be damn quick about it.'

Charlton didn't seem to have heard. He was holding the note again, lips moving slightly as he read.

'If I can't raise the money, they — they'll kill him.'

'I doubt it. They do that and there'll be no chance of them getting their hands on twenty-thousand dollars.'

It was pathetic to see the ray of hope flash across Linus's ravaged face. Cole looked away.

They might not *kill* Donny — but they could well begin mutilating him, send back an ear, or some fingers . . .

'What a helluva lousy deal,' he said aloud.

6

Turning Point

Bess was appalled at the news.

Linus was nervous and mumbled a lot and having to ask him to repeat everything made Bess really mad, jarred her out of her comfortless lethargy. Grief turned to anger.

'Kidnapped! My God, Linus! You've truly excelled yourself this time!'

'Are you mad, woman? It's not my fault! I specifically asked that damn sheriff to keep a special eye on Donny. If you're looking for someone to blame, blame Adam Cole!'

'Oh, I will — I do. But don't think it lets you off the hook!'

She started one of her tirades and Linus snapped, grabbed her by the shoulders — hurting his broken fingers but uncaring — and shook her until her head rocked violently on her shoulders. The words stopped and she looked startled, groped at him for support. He thrust her roughly from him and she stumbled back. She sat down heavily in an overstuffed armchair. She stared up at him apprehensively.

'You silly woman! This is no time to be looking for someone to blame! We have to get the ransom organized. You have to get Carl to send the money by telegraphic transfer or an authority for us to draw against the trust. I can arrange the bank's end of it but he'll have to expedite things. I haven't had a time limit named by the kidnappers but I'm sure it will be only a matter of days.'

His words got through and she realized the truth of what he said. 'Surely it will be faster for you to make some arrangement through the bank? Borrow the ransom?'

His face tightened and he shook his head. 'No. No, I don't want to ask this of head office. You've no idea the complicated procedure. An intensive investigation of us both — even an audit of our accounts. In fact they might choose to do a complete audit of the bank at the same time. I can't handle that and this crisis as well.'

'For heaven's sake, Linus! Tell them how urgent it is!'

Again he shook his head, his mouth a tight line. 'It will cut no ice, Bess, believe me. I know the system. It'll be much faster and satisfactory to have Carl wire us authority and put up the money. After all, it's for his nephew.'

Her damp eyes narrowed and she frowned. 'Is there something you haven't told me, Linus? Have you had . . . trouble with head office, over your books or some other . . . ?'

'Goddamnit, *no*! It's nothing like that. I just know what I'm dealing with here and it comes right down to this, Bess. If we want to see Donny alive again, we have to pay the ransom! Now, be sensible, get changed and I'll walk you down to the telegraph office so you can get some wires away to California.'

She sat there, hands clasped in her lap, fingers tearing at the delicate lace of a perfumed kerchief, looking up at him without a trace of affection.

'Of course I'll do this, Linus. But I still think it would be quicker for you to arrange it through the bank.'

'For God's sake, woman! *Will* you get changed!'

Breathing heavily, he started for the door.

'Your concern for Donny is admirable, Linus,' she said with heavy sarcasm. 'Considering how you feel about him.'

He paused, hand on the doorknob. 'He's only a boy, Bess. Give me some credit for genuine concern.'

'Well, I suppose there's a lot of guilt behind it. If not, there ought to be!'

He managed not to slam the door behind him.

★ ★ ★

It was the seventh of July.

Cole rode out of town early, headed for a place where he could overlook the river and the field where the Fourth's celebrations had taken place. There was a little activity there, a few men scouting around, looking for sign that might come in handy later.

He ought to be down there with them, he supposed, but — no. This was a special day to him and he preferred to be alone. Rolling a cigarette while sitting on a rock, his wounded leg straight out, boot resting a few inches above the ground between two rocks, he glanced at his grazing mount, a dappled grey mare. There was a bottle of bar whiskey in the saddlebags. It might be marginally better than the moonshine that had affected him so badly on Independence Day. Usually, he drank a full bottle, sometimes more, on July 7 — he had for the past five years, anyway.

But — maybe not today. Maybe it

was time to just sit and think and remember *why* . . .

★ ★ ★

He had been alone since he was a button. Dragged around the cattle trails by his widowed father from the age of four, virtually reared by trail cooks and rough cowboys.

His father was killed trying to stop a stampede when the boy was six and he was passed from hand to hand amongst the trail men. Fortunately, he was intelligent and learned something of the rugged, dangerous life. He could rope and brand and ride, repair wagons, skinout a slaughtered cow or a deer — many times the deer had been hunted, stalked and shot by him.

Ailing horses and cows frightened him at first but soon he learned how to treat their problems, or, if they weren't treatable, to put them out of their misery as painlessly as possible.

There were men who enjoyed watching animals suffer, he found. And there were men who made these sadistic types suffer, too. So, by watching, and later by experience, he learned how to use his fists — and later still, how to use his guns.

He was a natural good rifle shot. Once a well-known gunfighter rode with the herd for a few days — obviously on the run from the law — and when two representatives of that law caught up with him, Cole saw how the man had earned his reputation. He wounded both deputies and the trail boss, pretty damn courageously, after witnessing the speed of the gunfight, ran the *pistolero* off with a shotgun. He cared for the wounded lawmen, took a detour to a town so they could get proper medical attention.

'Weren't you scared, boss?' Cole had asked. 'I mean, you seen how fast he was with a gun and he was sure ready to use it . . .'

'Don't admire him, kid,' the trail boss

told him curtly. 'Bein' fast with a gun is nothin' much. You think such a man is popular. He ain't. A lot of the time, it's just that folk are plain scared of him, don't want to rub him up the wrong way. So they pretend to admire him. Oh, some actually do, of course, but all in all, bein' a gunfighter ain't anythin' to be proud of. Pride's for the man who earns the respect of his pards.'

Later, one of the wranglers told him that the boss had once been a gunfighter, but one of his bullets wounded a child and he hadn't worn a six-gun since; swore he never would.

A nighthawk was killed in an Indian raid one night and the trail boss handed the man's Colt rig to the boy — now approaching his teens.

'This is a good weapon, son. You need to carry one if you aim to follow the cattle trails.' The trail boss paused. 'You dunno nothin' about handguns, do you? You're OK with a rifle, but a Colt, no. Well, I'll teach you how to take 'em apart and put 'em back together blindfolded.'

'Why would I want to do it blindfolded?'

''Cause sometime you might be in a bind in the dark and you'll need to be able to recognize each part of your gun and its workin's by touch. Might never happen, but if it does . . . you get to see the sunrise.'

The trail boss, calling himself simply 'Montana' now, kept his word and Cole turned out to be a good pupil.

'Will you show me a fast draw?'

'Son, I will not. I'll show you a *safe* draw, so you don't shoot your own foot off or your hoss, or even your saddle mate if he's close by. But you won't need a lightnin'-quick draw.'

'How d'you know? S'pose I find I do need a slick draw — and can't do it. I'm dead.'

The trail boss, a grizzled man pushing sixty, worked his jaws on his chaw of tobacco and spat a stream, never taking his rheumy grey eyes off the youngster.

'Thing is, son, you can show a man all the short cuts you know — but it's up to him to use them as fast as he's able — and some men just ain't able. *That*'s what gets 'em killed: believin' they know how to make a slick draw — and when it comes down to doin' it the only fast thing they get is a funeral.'

But twice he caught the kid behind the chuck wagon, testing himself, whipping out his Colt from the dead nighthawk's rig. He was pretty good, but fumbled a lot. At last the boss took him aside.

'You disappoint me, boy. Why you so damn keen to learn how to draw fast?'

''Cause my father never could draw fast and it near got him killed when I was just a shaver. I was never so scared in my life, wonderin' if he'd die or recover.'

The trail boss frowned. 'Who looked after you while he was recoverin'?'

The kid looked at him steadily. 'I looked after myself. An' him, too. The man who shot him left us out in the desert.'

'He left you too?' The boss was outraged. 'By God, what kinda snake was he, this fast gun?'

The kid's gaze didn't waver. 'A dead one — eventually. After I caught up with him.'

'How old were you?'

Cole shrugged. 'I dunno — eight, mebbe, coulda been nine or ten . . . '

The trail boss didn't ask any more, but he took the Colt from the kid and showed him how his grip was wrong, how the holster was too low, and how cutting out a piece of leather to allow the finger to reach the trigger at the moment of draw was a definite advantage.

Once again, the kid was an apt pupil.

'I ever hear of you tryin' to make a name for yourself as a fast gun, I'll come after you. There's a trick or two I ain't taught you and it'll gimme the edge if I have to chase you down.'

★ ★ ★

Cole never went looking for trouble. Once or twice he had to put his acquired gun-speed to use. Mostly, if he used the Colt at all it was during a trail drive — or when doing ranch work. For he drifted around, took a variety of jobs, all connected with cattle. It was all he knew and he enjoyed the life, meeting the tough rannies who rode these trails, living out lonely winters in line shacks, talking to the cows and the wild animals on occasion, just to hear his own voice.

He knew women in the trail towns, he 'saw the elephant', but he often stared longingly at ranchers in from their spreads, with wives and families. He didn't recall his mother very well but he knew she had been soft and kind and had made him feel good.

But a wife and ranch was out of reach of a drifting trail hand who could barely write, like him. He knew that. The rough cowboys joshed him when they saw him in one of his dreamy moods.

'Cole, you ever see a rich cowboy? I mean for more'n a few days? If he's got money, he spends it, recovers from a bender and lousy hangover, then what does he do? Go trailin' again, works his butt off, and does the same blame thing all over ... *That*'s a cowboy's life. There ain't many married ones. I mean, what woman'd want a man who wasn't gonna sit across the supper table from her more'n a coupla times a year?'

So he started saving his money. Sure, he painted a few towns red with his pards, but he had an arrangement with a small bank in Denver where he could deposit money by telegraph. At trail's end, on pay-day, his first stop was at a telegraph station where he laboriously filled out the necessary forms and got his bank account number from the greasy slip of paper a clerk had written it on for him and sent off a few dollars.

Those of the crew who knew, joshed him, often asked him for a loan, but knew it would never be forthcoming.

They made fun of him but he had the

last laugh: he met Alice Brown in a town where the herd was flood-bound for two weeks.

At the end of that time, he quit the trail herd and the boss was generous enough to pay him the bonus he would've earned if he had completed the drive.

He and Alice were married and he took up a quarter-section and homesteaded it. They had a boy child, named him Jeff, after Alice's dead father, and Cole knew he had found what he had been searching for all those years without even realizing it: happiness and comfort in the form of a beautiful, loving woman, a healthy son and a small ranch that would soon expand. *Satisfaction*, that's what it was; at long last he had found himself a satisfactory life.

Then three days after the community had celebrated one Independence Day, some kids playing with left-over fireworks shot a rocket into a loaded haywagon parked against the west wall of the log house.

Cole was out on the range, fencing, when he first saw the smoke. He hit the saddle at a dead run and rode straight as an arrow towards the flames he could now see shooting up above the hogback rise.

It was too late. A warped door he had been meaning to fix had jammed and Alice and the boy had been overcome by smoke. Although the neighbours had the fire out quickly, it wasn't quick enough to save his family.

The boy would have been six years old now, his birthday being the Seventh of July.

Instead of celebrating the boy's progress through life, for the past five years Adam Cole had drunk himself senseless each July 7, drowning thoughts of what might have been . . .

But not this time!

This time he could do something about *saving* a boy and he would need to be as sober as a bishop.

In a moment of new resolve he took

the whiskey bottle and smashed it against the rocks. He watched the dark-brown liquid trickle away, soak into the earth.

Whether he were successful in finding Donny Charlton, or not, he realized he had reached some kind of turning point this day.

The tragedies and happiness of the past were still there. Nothing had changed, never could change.

But he could.

And this was the time.

7

The Strangers

It was after sundown on July 8 when Cole rode slowly back into town, the weary grey plodding towards the livery. The hostler helped him down from the saddle and the sheriff, grimy from long trails, leaned against the stall post and massaged his aching leg.

'How's the wound comin', Cole?'

'I can tell you it's still there,' the sheriff growled, then smiled crookedly, softening his tone. 'It's not too bad, Earl. If those hardcases hadn't massaged it with their boots I'd be running like a deer now.'

The hostler nodded soberly, took his pipe from his leathery lips, sniffed deeply through his bulbous nose. 'They was strangers, but I think I've seen the one in the green shirt before. Rode in with that Quinlan feller few days earlier but stayed on for the Fourth.'

That news earned the livery man a sharp look. 'Why the hell didn't you tell me? I've covered half the damn county these past couple of days, trying to get a line on him and his pard. Reckon they're connected to the kidnapping.'

The hostler sniffed again, moved his feet uneasily. 'Well, I dunno who he is, Cole. Just recollected he came in with Quinlan.'

'Yeah, all right, Earl. Take care of the horse.'

As the sheriff took down his rifle and warbag, Earl said, 'Linus asked me to tell you, when you showed he wants to see you.' He paused, then added, 'Poor devil looks like death warmed over. 'Course, that Bess ain't makin' things any easier for him.'

Cole nodded and headed back to his room at the Star. He ordered hot water for a bath and afterwards shaved. Halfway through there was a knock on the door and Linus Charlton came hurrying in.

'I've had a second note,' he said, without preamble. He produced a crumpled piece of paper and offered it to Cole.

The sheriff saw it was the same printing as before:

Better hurry with that money
This is just to show we really
do have the kid.
Next time it could be a finger

Linus held up a tuft of greasy, tow-coloured hair. 'All Bess said was 'They might've let him wash his hair!'' He shook his head jerkily, his drawn, greyish face tightening. 'Damn woman.'

The banker looked terrible: he had dark smears under his eyes, his jowls were drooping, even his neck seemed scrawny. He still wore a bandage on his left hand and it looked to be the same grimy one from a couple of days ago.

'Where've you been, Cole? Damnit, man, I need to have you close by for this thing.'

'Rode around to see everyone I could remember being at the celebration and who didn't come from town. Didn't learn much. Most folk saw Donny and some playmate, Sam Bale, but no one saw them leave the area. Didn't get as far out as the Bale place or the Bowden spread, but I'll take a packhorse later and cover more ground.'

'Well, I dunno how much more time they aim to give me to get the ransom. I'd be obliged if you'd stay close.'

'Linus, you do your part with the ransom. I'll do what I can from my side. Have you got the OK for the money yet?'

Charlton heaved a sigh. 'Yes — and no. I mean, Carl Curtis, after a slew of wires sent in Bess's name, finally agreed to allow access to the trust funds — but it's gotta be done through my bank's head office. The very thing I was trying to avoid!'

Cole frowned. 'Makes it easier, doesn't it?'

'You might think so.' There was a dull sound to Linus's words. 'Now, as well as all this worry, and making the arrangements, I have to write *reports* which amount to little more than 'Please Explain' — and that's ridiculous. What can you say about a kidnapping, other than it happened?' He rubbed hard at his head, shaking it. 'I haven't slept more than two hours straight since I last saw you.'

'Looks like it, too. Linus, you'd better take or, better still, *make* time so you have a break. Once they want the ransom, you'll be working like a berserk beaver and its just the time you'll need all your wits about you. If you don't get it right, for some reason . . .'

Linus nodded. 'I know. Bess blames me — oh, you, too, equally, I think. She's relentless in her criticism. I — I even hoped at one stage that the kid would turn up — dead. Just to have the blasted thing finished with.'

'You wouldn't want that to happen,' Cole said slowly and Linus knew *he* meant he wouldn't want it to happen, either.

He didn't know about Cole's past and the loss of his own son five years earlier, but for some time he had suspected a tragedy somewhere along Cole's backtrail.

'When will you have the money ready?'

'If I can stall head office on these unnecessary 'reports', tomorrow afternoon, maybe. I — I'm going to count it myself and package it. That way there'll be no mistakes, and it should keep those fools in Denver off my neck.'

'You ought to have someone with you to check, Linus. That's what will keep head office off you. And it'll be better if anyone claims there's been a mistake.'

'No! I *want* to do this myself as far as possible, Cole. I have to square myself with Bess and if I can take credit for getting the ransom paid and bringing Donny back safely . . . '

Cole could see the man's reasoning: he was probably more afraid of Bess than of his superiors in Denver but he would never admit it.

'Cole, I need to ask you another favour.' The sheriff waited, face unreadable. 'Will — will you deliver the ransom? Oh, I know there're no arrangements yet, but — well, you're experienced in handling this kind of thing.'

'No, I'm not, Linus. I've never been involved in a kidnapping pay-off. But if they're agreeable to me handing over the ransom, I'll do it.'

He was surprised at the relief that showed on the banker's face. It seemed the man was close to collapse and now some of the tension drained away — visibly.

'I — I'm much obliged, Cole, very much obliged.'

Then Linus wheeled and fumbled at the door, and stumbled out into the passage, leaving the door swinging.

Cole slowly closed it, frowning.

★ ★ ★

Because payment instructions for the ransom seemed imminent, Sheriff Cole did not make his planned extended ride out to the edges of the county, interviewing people who had attended the Independence Day celebrations.

As Banker Charlton had pointed out, when instructions came they would likely have to be acted upon pronto. Linus was ready to go, now that the bank's head office had at last approved release of the money. In fact the Denver people sent extra funds down in a strongbox on a special stage run, to supplement what Linus's safe already held. $20,000 was one hell of a lot of money.

No wonder Denver was nervous.

Cole had escorted the strongbox from the depot to the bank and then Linus locked himself in his office, preparing the ransom, taking full responsibility.

Feeling edgy, with it being more or

less general knowledge that part of the ransom had arrived and was being counted in the bank, Cole stayed in town, on the balcony outside his hotel room. Using field glasses he watched the bank and its surrounds, noting everyone who entered the building.

He was bored after a while but admitted the enforced rest was helping his leg's recovery. He barely limped at all now, though he couldn't run yet — jog-trot for a short distance, maybe, but no more.

He swept the glasses around town and some of the country that he could see beyond the outskirts. The lenses were good quality, Army issue, but still not good enough to pick out the features of riders approaching the town, entering by way of the short adobe bridge at the southern end of Front Street.

That was how he missed recognizing the two men who drifted in, several minutes apart. One was forking a big black, the other a dirty-white gelding.

They both made for the livery and he moved the glasses back to the bridge trail, then slowly around the outskirts.

He jumped when shortly afterwards a piping voice behind him called his name. 'Sher'f Cole . . . ?'

He spun round, regretting it as pain shot through his leg. He stared at a freckle-faced boy in ragged patched overalls, only one strap holding the garment up.

'What d'you want, son?'

'I'm Toddy. My father runs the stables. He sent me to find you.'

'What's up, Toddy?'

'He said to tell you that the feller in the green shirt's just arrived — only he ain't wearin' a green shirt today. It's faded blue. And he was ridin' a black geldin'.'

Cole was tense. 'Where is he?'

'Turned his mount in for groomin'. Pa's doin' it — '

'Was he alone?'

The kid scratched his head — another towhead, Cole noticed. The town seemed full of them. 'Might've been someone with him — another feller arrived a coupla minutes after him. He had a grey shirt an' was wearin' a tatty old vest over it. I — I think they knew each other, but din' let on, you know?'

'You're pretty bright, Toddy, noticing something like that. You couldn't be mistaken?'

'No, sir. Not the way they looked at each other and the one in the blue shirt kind of — nodded, but hardly moved his head. Like this.'

Cole gave the boy a dime and, as the kid ran off down the length of the balcony, went into his room and picked up his rifle from where he had left it in a corner.

He locked the door behind him and hurried down the stairs into the hotel foyer.

Using the back alleys, he made his way to the law office, entered by the rear door and placed his rifle beside the battered desk; if the men he wanted to see saw him walking the streets with a rifle in hand, they might be scared off.

And he didn't want that: he wanted to know what they were up to. Someone had to deliver those ransom notes.

* * *

It was approaching sundown and long shadows began to mottle the streets. Men who worked in town at the stores and the small sawmill, the stage depot and so on, closed up shop and many of them made their way to Mannering's Delta saloon to sink a few beers and maybe a whiskey, if they could afford it, before heading home to supper.

Cole felt like a drink, had done for a couple of days, but hadn't been game to give in. He was still afraid he might capitulate and throw his annual drunk — he sure had his head full of Alice and Jeff. It was normal for him at this time of year, but with the ransom payment looming, he couldn't afford any diversions.

Still, he entered the saloon, scanned the drinkers at the bar and the tables scattered around the smoky room. The men Toddy had warned him about, Blue Shirt and Vest, as he thought of them, were sitting at a table near a side door. He let his gaze slide across them without pause.

He greeted a few townsfolk, breasted the bar and ordered a beer, using the large mirror to watch the two men who claimed his interest. They, in turn, were surreptitiously watching him, but he merely leaned an elbow on the counter and rolled a cigarette, chatting with one of the sweating barkeeps. He lit up and shook out the vesta, eyes still a little dazzled by the brief flare of the match.

A glance in the mirror showed him the two men had gone. Smart! They'd waited until the match briefly blinded him and then left, quickly and silently. It had to be by the side door . . .

Cole crossed swiftly to a table where four townsmen were laughing over a joke one of them had just told. It was only a few feet from the side door.

'Two rannies just go out?' he asked and the laughter died slowly.

A big man in sweat-stained shirt, his chair facing the door nodded. 'Coupla strangers, Sheriff.'

'Blue shirt? Other with a vest over grey?'

The man was still nodding when Cole crossed to the door in two fast strides, then changed his mind and hurried down the smoke-filled room to the front batwings. He shouldered past a couple of men on their way in, ignoring the curses, moved quickly to the corner of the building.

There was no sign of his quarry in the now darkened alley. Darting his gaze about, he searched for places they might have gone. There were two lanes, one curving back to Front Street about a block along from the saloon. The other led to a secondary street, down past the general store, skirted the yard behind the saddler's and then swung towards the block where the bank stood.

And the side with the special door leading to Charlton's office faced onto it.

Cole drew his Colt, automatically checking the loads by turning the cylinder slowly and feeling the noses of the bullets in the chambers with his fingertip. While doing this, he watched for the men.

There was movement between him and the bank door, just a formless shadow, but it was too big to be that of a pariah dog or an alley cat. He padded forward, walking on the balls of his feet. It was a strain on his left leg but he gritted his teeth against the cramping pain. Only a few more steps and he would have the drop on them.

It was just a faint sound, very brief, as something whispered through the air. His reactions, he thought later, were as good as they had ever been, despite any residual hangover from that poisonous moonshine.

He propped and the descending gun clipped the brim of his hat. He lurched sideways as the man who had tried to drop him cold stumbled forward with the motion of the swinging weapon. Cole smashed his Colt into the side of the attacker's head, knocking off his hat. The man grunted and fell to the ground where his hat was already rolling in the dust.

His companion, near the bank door, heard the sounds and rounded fast, his gun firing, the flash briefly outlining him, clearly enough to show the faded blue colour of his shirt.

Cole triggered and his bullet knocked the man spinning. He crashed into the bank door, clawed at the wood and sat down, one leg bent under him. His head rested against the woodwork, his body jamming one arm. The other was clawing at his chest.

He froze when Cole's gun muzzle pressed into his grimy neck.

Just then a startled, eye-popping Linus Charlton wrenched open the door, gun in one hand, some banknotes in the other. 'What the devil . . . ?'

'Open the door wider, Linus. We've got two of 'em to drag in. With a little luck, it'll be an interesting conversation.'

'No!' The small-calibre handgun lifted and covered the surprised lawman. 'Sorry, Cole. No one comes into my office while I'm counting the ransom — and that includes you. If you want to question these two, take 'em down to your jail.'

The door slammed and the key turned in the lock.

The gunfire had attracted some curious folk, mostly drinkers from the saloon, and Cole organized four of them to bring the strangers down to the law office.

The wounded man was gasping that he needed a sawbones, he was dying.

'Then what you need is an undertaker,' Cole said flatly. 'You'll get medical attention in the cells. Fry, will you go get Doc Partridge and send him along?'

The townsman nodded and broke

away from the small group following Cole. The man the sheriff gunwhipped was starting to groan and move a little but was still mighty groggy.

Until they reached the landing at the front door of the law office and Cole fumbled out his keys.

Then the man in the frayed vest suddenly came to life, kicking one of the men half-carrying him, smashing his forehead into the face of the second man, who lurched back, yelling, blood spraying. There was a tangle and Cole was knocked against the door, pinned briefly by the stumbling men.

Others were shouting but all dived for cover as the man in the grey shirt pulled his gun and started shooting. A townsman dropped without a sound and another gave a cry of pain. The rest either hit the dirt or ran for whatever cover they could find.

The fugitive loosed two shots at Cole, making him duck. While the sheriff did that, trying to shoot past some of the weaving townsmen, the vest man leapt into the saddle of a horse at a nearby hitchrack and spurred away.

Cole jumped over prostrate townsmen, raised his Colt but swore as he was forced to hold his fire. The runaway was weaving in between the evening traffic and didn't offer a clear shot.

'Lock that *hombre* in the cell when the doc's finished with him,' he ordered as he started to run for a tethered horse. Pain immediately knifed through his leg and he staggered. But he was able to slap the reins loose and ram his left foot into the stirrup. His leg collapsed again and the horse whinnied and shied, throwing him.

Dimly, he heard the drumming of the other horse's hoofs as it sped over the bridge.

Cursing, a couple of townsmen helped get him into the saddle, ignoring yells from the horse's owner. He spurred after the fugitive, noting with satisfaction that there was a rifle in the saddle scabbard.

It was about as dark as it was going

to get now and he had to rely on his ears to follow the escaping gunman. They were into the trees here, weaving between the trunks. Branches scraped his shoulders as he lay low in the saddle. He reined down, the horse blowing, his heart slamming against his ribs. He couldn't hear the other mount!

Rifle in hand now, he eased the horse forward slowly, using his heels and knees to guide it; luckily it was a cow pony, used to such commands. Then flame stabbed out of the darkness to his right: *that son of a bitch had set up an ambush!*

The lead was close and he slid from the saddle, dancing on his good leg. He slapped the horse's rump, sending it racing on. The gun followed its sound, firing again.

Cole threw up the rifle, triggered at the flash, slightly up and to the left. He heard a grunt and a thrashing, and though he waited, there was no more shooting.

8

Closing In

'Am I gonna die, Doc?'

Partridge straightened and pressed one hand into his aching back, dropping bloody rags into a bucket on the cell floor.

'Well, I wouldn't say . . . '

Cole, leaning against the end of the bunk in the cell, cleared his throat. The sound caught the doctor's attention and he paused. Cole shook his head slightly: *Don't tell him he's not going to die!*

Partridge knew what the lawman wanted from years of similar situations and turned again to the wounded man with the bandaged chest, stretched out on the bunk.

'I wouldn't say you were a good candidate for any long-term life insurance. Sorry, but I've done all I can.'

The man still had a black eye and a scabbed gash on his cheek from the fight with Cole on the Fourth of July. His skin was greyish and there was fear in his eyes. He pawed the doctor's arm as Partridge gathered his instruments and lotions.

'Doc, I — I can't breathe!' His chest was heaving but Partridge winked at Cole with the eye the wounded man couldn't see. He mouthed the word 'panic', but said aloud,

'Just lie quiet, son. It'll make the passing a lot easier. No sense in getting fussed at a time like this.'

'Oh, God!' The eyes were wide now, sought out the hard-faced Cole who was casually rolling a cigarette. 'I'm too young to die!'

'What are you? Twenty-four, twenty-five? Hell, I seen boys sixteen, *fourteen*, die in my squad durin' the War.'

'I'm twenny-six! An' I don't wanna die!'

Cole shrugged, held the cell door open for the medic to pass through into the passage. 'That's just what your pard said after I shot him in the trees earlier.'

From the passage, the doctor said, 'Best make a clean breast of your sins, son. Smoothe the way some. You'll feel better, with your conscience clear. I won't bother you with the undertaker right now. In the morning'll do.'

Partridge moved away down the passage and the wounded man rolled his head, began to cough, clasping his chest.

'What's your name?' Cole asked, as he finished making the cigarette and fumbled out a match.

'Larry Creed.'

'You like a last cigarette, Larry?' Cole held out the one he had just lit. 'Then again, guess it might tear up your lungs, and we're trying to make things easier for you. But it's really up to you to help yourself.'

Creed stared, wide-eyed, mouth working soundlessly.

Cole, starting to turn away, suddenly swung back. 'You really want to unload yourself, Larry? Get some of your bad doings off your chest?'

Creed continued to stare, but when Cole shrugged and began to leave, he rasped, 'Wait up! Don't leave me to die alone.'

'Sorry, Larry. I've got a lot of paperwork to do. I'd like to oblige you, but I guess it's too late for that. I'll give you a little privacy. A man should take time to think about things when he's like you are, so close to goin'.'

'Er — no. I wouldn't mind you — stayin'. We could talk — for a bit.'

Cole frowned, looked uncertain. 'Well, I dunno. I've got a lot of things on my mind right now, too. Like Donny Charlton's kidnapping, and the ransom. I really don't think I can afford the time to just sit here and — '

'I — I can tell you somethin' about the kid.' Creed was eager, half-risen off the bunk now, convinced he would be dead before morning, wanting company right to the last.

'I don't even know who took him.'

'Aw, we got him. I mean me an' Mitch — my pard you just killed — and a coupla other fellers.'

'Tells me nothing. *Where?*'

'Well, we holed up in a crooked canyon in the Flintrocks.'

'That's a helluva big place, Larry!'

'Yeah — we just stumbled on the place. Damn good hideout — almost at the base of the Church Spire. Know it?'

Cole did: it was a high column of basalt, tapering to a point like the spire on a church. He said nothing, drew on his cigarette, looking bored. Sitting on the edge of the bunk opposite Creed's, he moved restlessly, as if he was thinking of moving. Creed ran a tongue around his lips, his only thought that he didn't want to die alone; he was *eager* to talk so that Cole would stay put.

'Quinlan's behind it,' he gasped suddenly and the sheriff had to stop himself from revealing how interested he was in this piece of information.

'You're joshing me. I mean, what the hell would a man like Quinlan want to kidnap Donny Charlton for?'

Creed almost smiled. 'Got you interested now, huh? Well, Quinlan's havin' trouble with Devlin. Wants more money and Devlin won't cough up. So he got this idea of kidnappin' Charlton's brat. You know — a bank president, rich wife. They ought to be willin' to pay up, he figures. An' plenty.'

'Well, twenty thousand's sure a heap of money.' Cole hoped he spoke with the right amount of reverence.

Creed did smile now, not noticing any pain, having virtually forgotten his wound. 'Shucks — that's only the start!'

'What d'you mean?'

'They pay up, but Quinlan holds onto the kid — asks for another twenty thousand. You get it?'

Cole got it, all right. It was the kind of lousy deal Quinlan would pull. 'When's the ransom got to be paid? And how?'

'Ask Charlton. He's got all the details.'

Suddenly Creed narrowed his eyes,

felt the bandages covering his chest wound. He rubbed them gently, frowned, staring at Cole. Then his face blackened as a thundercloud settled above it. *He wasn't feeling any worse!*

'Just a minute, you miserable son of a bitch. I ain't dyin' at all, am I! You and that stinkin' sawbones — you blame well *tricked* me! Judas priest — ' His chest was heaving now with emotion. His words began to tumble over themselves, his anger so great he didn't finish all the syllables in one word before trying to spit out another.

'I've heard of fellers getting delirious just before they die, Larry. You best go easy. You're talking gibberish.'

'Christ, Cole! If I had a gun! A club! *Anythin'*! I'd pound your head flat!'

'Bet you would, too. Why'd you and Mitch come to Barberry? You bring another note?'

'Go ride off a cliff! I wish we'd kicked your face in at the hoedown!'

'You seem to've recovered pretty well, Larry.' Cole dropped the cigarette and crushed it under a boot. 'Guess you ain't gonna tell me anything else, but I know a bit more now. You'll live to hang yet.'

Creed tried to struggle off the bunk as Cole unlocked the door and stepped out of the cell, but he *was* hurt, though far from fatally, and he sagged back, gasping. He swore savagely as the key turned in the lock.

'You — you ain't gettin' away with this, Cole, damn your eyes!'

'Maybe you better not kick up too big a fuss, Creed. If Quinlan gets to hear we got you prisoner, and *wounded* . . . Yeah, that's better. Relax. Someone'll bring you breakfast come morning. Now, get yourself a good night's sleep.'

Grating curses followed the sheriff all the way down to the front office.

★ ★ ★

'What the hell did Creed mean, saying you had all the details about paying the

129

ransom, Linus?'

Cole glared down at the banker seated behind his desk, the piles of money covered with a green-baize cloth. Charlton looked highly nervous in the lamplight. He fiddled with the wick control, sat back, then immediately leaned forward and slopped some whiskey into a glass. He tossed it down, coughed once, looked hard at the sheriff.

'You want one, you'll have to drink from the bottle. I don't have another glass.'

'I don't want any, Linus — and you better quit. You make a mistake with your figures counting that money and you *will* be in a heap of trouble with your head office.'

It had taken a threat of blowing the lock off Linus's office door with a shotgun before the rattled banker would open up and allow the sheriff to enter.

'Creed says you know about paying the ransom. How? And I mean 'how do you know'?'

Charlton started to reach for the bottle again, changed his mind. He seemed to make a decision — or just remembered something. He reached into a desk drawer, waved a creased and grimy sheet of paper at Cole.

'I found this after I'd closed the side door on you earlier. Creed or Mitch must've pushed it under just before you jumped them.'

Cole frowned. Well, it sure wasn't Mitch — he was much too far away. But had Creed been close enough to push the note under the door? Hard to tell in the semi-dark, and then Mitch had tried to club him, and there was shooting . . .

Cole took the paper and smoothed it on the banker's desk. He recognized the same printing as on the previous notes.

Tomorrow night. Right after moonset Birdwing Wells. North edge. Round rock broke on one side leave money under then get out we'll be watching If money OK kid'll be returned

Cole blew out his cheeks, looking at Linus as he downed another whiskey. 'Sounds like a Quinlan deal.'

Charlton started, suddenly wild-eyed. 'Quinlan? What's he got to do with it . . . ?'

Cole told him about Creed. 'Scared he was dying, didn't want me to leave, spilled his guts. Up to a point.'

'Oh, God! A man like Quinlan, holding Donny's life in his hands.'

'A man like what, Linus? You admitting you know Quinlan now?'

Linus slumped, nodded miserably. He held up his bandaged hand. 'He did this. A warning from Brack Devlin.'

'Guessed as much. But a warning about what?'

Linus stared blankly, then swallowed yet another drink. Cole leaned forward and took the bottle. The banker looked as if he would protest but changed his mind.

'Stay sober, you damn fool!'

Charlton slumped, not looking at the sheriff. He sighed heavily.

'All right. I'm something of a gambler on the quiet.'

'Not so quiet, Linus. I've known for months about your losses in Mannering's back room.'

This brought Linus's head up. His jaw dropped. 'You — you're full of surprises, Cole!'

'But you losing money to Mannering — how does that have anything to do with Brack Devlin?'

'They work for the same group back East. A group of hardheads own big pieces of their saloons, and a lot of others, I hear. Devlin's sort of a — a collector. He's told about who owes money — '

'And who's behind in paying up?'

Linus swallowed and nodded miserably. 'They think because I'm president of this bank I can lay my hands on money at any time! That's why they gave me so much easy credit. Damn fools! I have to account for every cent!'

'You're mighty foolish gambling at all in your position, Linus.'

'I've heard it all before, Cole! So don't waste your breath.' The banker spoke tersely and then scrubbed a hand down his sweating face. 'I — I've tried to keep it from Bess. I hinted I needed some money but she's determined I'll never get my hands on a single dollar of her legacy.' He shook his head jerkily, compressed his lips. 'I could *kill* her at times! Anyway, to my surprise, after I explained to Mannering how I couldn't come up with what I owed right away, Quinlan suddenly appeared on my doorstep and made the most outrageous threats. All smiles and pleasant while he did so, which made them worse, if anything! Then he suddenly grabbed my left hand and — and broke my two middle fingers! I couldn't believe it was happening to me — in my own office! He clapped a hand over my mouth as I started to yell, banged my head back against the chair, then threw me on the floor and placed his boot across my throat. Still speaking calmly, he told me to either pay the money within one week or they'd find a way to make me pay up.'

'You didn't pay, so they kidnapped Donny and now demand twenty thousand in ransom. How much do you owe?'

'That's — that's none of your business, Cole!'

'I think it is, but let it go. You've been an awful damn fool, Linus. But I'll stick by my word and handle the ransom payment for you.'

For a moment he thought the rattled banker was going to cry but the man regained control, cleared his throat and looked longingly at the bottle in Cole's hands. The sheriff gave it to him and Linus drank straight from the neck.

'All right, Linus, let's get started and work out some kind of plan.'

'They've — already made the plan!'

'Their plan isn't necessarily mine.'

'Cole! You've got to do just as they say! Otherwise — you don't know what they'll do to Donny!'

'Or me if I ride in blind, hoping they'll stick to their side of things. It's all pretty damn risky, but I aim to come out of this alive, Linus.'

The banker put his head in his hands.

9

Old Enemies

Cole hired Josh and Joel Miller as temporary deputies, leaving them to watch the town — and Creed in the jail cell, with instructions to call Doc Partridge if necessary.

He hired a fresh mount from the livery, a strong-willed, hard-muscled black gelding with a wary eye and big, ready teeth.

'He'll run from here to next Tuesday week without falterin', long as you don't rake him with your spurs,' Earl the livery man assured Cole. 'Dig them rowels in too deep an' you'll be lookin' at the world from the top of the nearest tree — if he don't buck you clear over it.'

Cole must have looked uncertain, for the hostler added, 'I know you treat

137

hosses OK, Cole. An' this one'll serve you well. My word on it.'

He also hired a packhorse, bought some supplies, including spare ammunition and shells for a sawn-off shotgun that came with the sheriff's job.

When he went to Linus Charlton's office to pick up the ransom money he found the banker nervous and looking more than usually worried.

'It's not even noon, Cole! They said moonset, which won't be till after midnight.'

'I don't aim to keep to their timetable, Linus.'

'What the hell're you planning?'

'Just to arrive early and get the lie of things.'

'Damnit, Cole, don't you do anything that'll put Donny in danger!'

'Linus, he's already in danger. I won't take any chances of him coming to harm, but I don't aim to arrive in the dark. If I can, I'll save you that ransom money.'

Linus dropped into his desk chair,

shaking his head, face white and sweating with strain. 'Will you please get it through your head that the *money's not important*! Let them have it! Just — just bring Donny back safely. I'm warning you, Cole, if anything happens to that boy because of you — well, I won't be answerable for your fate.'

Cole didn't smile, although Linus did seem a mite comical with his rotund figure, trying to bluster and sound tough. But the poor devil must be churning up inside, blood pressure off the scale, maybe not too far from a heart attack.

'Linus, you have my word I won't endanger Donny. Is the money ready?'

'Of course it's ready.' The banker went to his private wall safe in one corner of the office, opened it and brought out a scratched leather valise. It bulged and there was a twist of wire with a lead bank seal through the strap and its buckle.

Cole frowned. 'I would've liked to've

checked it myself, Linus. Don't look like that! I'm putting my life on the line to deliver it, and if there's been any mistake — '

'There is no mistake!' The banker was short of breath now, he waved a heavy arm as if brushing away a blue-tailed fly. 'Just go, Cole. I'm sorry if I seem unreasonable but I've never been under such a strain.' He glanced up with a mild twitch of his bloodless lips. 'I have this vision of Bess waiting to hear — with a large, razor-sharp knife in her hands, ready to emasculate me . . .'

Poor devil: that woman had him whipped. Cole picked up the briefcase with one hand, noting its weight, and with the other clapped Linus briefly on his hunched shoulders.

'I should be back by sun up — with Donny.'

'I — I haven't prayed in years, but now I find myself constantly muttering a prayer that the kid'll be — all right.'

Charlton's haunted gaze stayed with

Cole all the way back to where he had tethered his horses outside the law office.

Josh Miller came out onto the landing, watched him ram the valise under his warbag on the black. 'Luck, Cole.'

The sheriff nodded. 'Josh, you recollect what Donny was wearing at the Fourth's hoe-down? I wasn't tracking too well that day but I seem to recollect denim trousers and some sort of moccasins, and a cloth cap, but I can't get a picture of his shirt.'

'Kinda grey — he had that checked jacket of his to wear for the night show; maybe he had it on and you didn't notice the shirt. Oh, yeah, he give the jacket to young Sam Bale after he fell in the river, Sam havin' a bad cold an' all. Dunno if Donny had it on again when he went missin'.'

Mounted now, Cole nodded, lifted a hand briefly as Joel appeared beside his brother. They didn't look in the least alike except from behind: they both had red hair and the same-shaped head.

'Creed's complainin' he's dyin' again, Cole.'

'Might as well fetch the doc. But Creed's sneaky, so be careful going into the cell with him. *Adios*, boys.'

They watched him ride down Front, leading his packhorse, and cross over the bridge. Then Joel started for Doc Partridge's and Josh went back into the cool of the office, starting to roll a cigarette.

Playing deputy was going to be a couple of days of easy money, he reckoned. A breeze.

★ ★ ★

Cole wasn't sure now whether he believed Larry Creed's story.

Quinlan *could* have set up the kidnapping off his own bat, but it was more likely that Brack Devlin had devised it as a way of recovering whatever money Linus owed Mannering, and, therefore, Devlin, as he was the Denver group's gambling controller for the area.

Linus was an utter fool for gambling when he was in such a position of trust. If ever there was a sum of money not accounted for at the bank, he would be immediately under suspicion. He might think his superiors didn't know about his weakness, but Cole figured those hard-nosed bankers would keep their fingers on the pulse of all their branches — and the men who ran them.

In any case, Quinlan was involved now, whether on Devlin's orders or operating on his own. And he was a mighty dangerous man, was 'Quick' Quinlan.

Cole had had a run-in with him about six months back when he was working for Careful Carmody, driving a freight wagon. Carmody was a twenty-mule-team man from way back who had had enough savvy to change the mules for four wheels and a six-horse team that could be increased to eight if the load demanded it. The mule teams had been too big an attraction for wandering Indians, who saw the little animals only as food on the hoof.

They were shipping-in gambling equipment for Brack Devlin's new casino at the time: imported roulette wheels, fancy card-tables with hidden slides that could work in the house's favour with a little practice and know-how, dice tables, even a gilt-edged piano, beds and ornate chairs; thousands of dollars' worth of high-class fittings for the new gambling and pleasure house.

Carmody's freight line had been free of raids by Indians since doing away with the mule teams. But the three wagons bound for Banjo Springs were close to their destination when a bunch of tiswin-crazed braves broke out of the new reservation at Greaswood Mesa.

The wagons lumbering across the wasteland, with only two outriders, were too big a temptation to pass up. The whole bunch, a round dozen in all, came screaming out of the sun as the freighters whipped and cursed their straining teams up the slope of a naked hogback rise.

The big mistake the renegades made was not riding around so they could attack coming *over* the rise, with the wagons below them. Instead, minds still fogged with tizwin fumes, they rode in across the flats, whooping and screaming, and had to put their mounts up the slope to reach the wagons.

Carmody, living up to his name, made no attempt to try to outrun the raiders; a blind man could see that would be futile. Instead, he signalled for the wagons to turn across the slope, and when they did, managing it just as the raiders came within gunshot range, the outriders started shooting while the drivers grabbed their guns.

Carmody had hired tough men, outriders and drivers paid double because of their reputations with firearms. Before the renegades could scatter, three of them crashed off their mounts, two not moving again, the third crawling away, trying to hold his stomach in; he didn't crawl far.

The renegades were no doubt shocked and the rush of adrenaline helped clear their brains. They scattered, some riding up and around to get above the wagons. Cole brought down two men and three horses with his Winchester. Three got through and had the advantage of shooting down into the wagons. The third driver, a man named McLaren, was wounded badly in the chest, but when a painted rider hauled alongside to climb aboard, McLaren shot him in the face with his six-gun. Bullets thudded into the wooden frames, and also into some of the merchandise. Even above the gunfire, Cole heard the new piano with the gingerbread gilt on the top give a loud, musical twang! as lead tore through the works. *Oh-oh!*

An outrider went down. Careful Carmody reeled as a bullet clipped one ear and blood sprayed from the mangled lobe. Cole had the heel shot off one boot but now the freighters were putting up such a withering fire with their repeating weapons that the surviving renegades, sobering by this time, lost their initial impetus and fell back, turned tail and limped away.

The wounded driver was attended to while Carmody examined the freight. He came back looking mighty worried.

'Devlin ain't gonna be happy,' was all he said, but a glance at the bullet-damaged freight was all that was needed to know that that was one hell of an understatement.

★　★　★

Brack Devlin was a smallish man with a narrow, hard face and deadly looking dark eyes. He was clean-shaven and always smelled of bay rum or some exotic male cologne. He dressed neatly and fastidiously, hair trimmed weekly just so, or there was hell to pay. He wore spectacles for reading, gold-wire frames, and he took them off when he

heard the news about his freight
— perhaps afraid his instant anger
would steam up the lenses.

'You don't include the piano in the
list of damaged goods, I trust, Carmody?'

The freighter, a beefy man and tough
in his own right, nodded curtly, not
afraid of Devlin, but uncomfortable at
having to report such damage.

'Afraid so, Mr Devlin. Them renegades were lousy shots, and a lot of
lead riddled my wagons.'

'Damn your wagons! I've been
waiting for those goods for months! I've
got prospective clients coming in from
all over. Now you tell me my stuff is
ruined!'

'Well, it sure is shot-up pretty bad, I
have to admit, Mr Devlin, but I guess
tradesmen could fix most of them
things given time.'

'Oh, you do, huh? Where d'you think
I'll find a piano tuner in this town? This
Territory, for Chrissakes! Or a carpen-
ter who can locate the same kind of

wood for repairs? And who the hell is gonna pay for it!'

Carmody had been waiting for that; he brought out some folded sheets of paper from an inside jacket pocket. He shook desert dust from the papers as he smoothed them out.

'Well, this here's our contract, Mr Devlin, and you signed it. It says all goods carried at owner's risk, which means — '

'I know what it means, you son of a bitch! It means you think you're gonna stick me with the bill!'

'You can hardly blame me for a bunch of drunken Injuns — '

'You think not, huh? Well, you listen to me!' Brack Devlin yelled, rising out of his chair and leaning on his hands across the desk, face deep red. 'You're gonna pay the bill! No, don't try to worm outta this, Carmody! You weren't careful enough this time, not dealing with *me*! I trusted you to bring them things down from Denver and all you've delivered is a pile of junk!'

He was yelling really loudly now. The door opened quickly and Quinlan stepped in, one hand on his gun butt. He was like a barrel with legs, a *big* barrel, and his head rested on top of wide shoulders like a balanced cannon ball. He had jet-black sideburns, and his curly black hair came low on his forehead. Bushy eyebrows jutted above deep sockets and cold brown eyes stared out like gun barrels.

Well-trained, eager for violence, Quinlan headed straight for the freighter, coming in like a bull buffalo.

Careful Carmody grew careless, tried to ease his six-gun out of leather on the side away from the man. Quinlan towered over him, and slammed *his* Colt barrel across the freighter's head. The big man caught him easily as his legs folded, heaved him over one shoulder, turned to look at the fuming Devlin.

'What about his crew?'

'You know what to do. Now go and do it. And burn the bastard's wagons for good measure. If I'm not going to get dollar-one outta him, I'll see him ruined as well as crippled by the time I'm through.'

Quinlan grinned in anticipation and strode towards the door . . .

Cole had been at the livery, arranging corral space for the teams, and now headed back to the freight depot, crossing a vacant lot and coming up on it from the rear.

He almost stumbled over the body of the other driver — the wounded one was at the local infirmary — sprawled in the long grass. The man was a mess, face barely visible behind a mask of blood, nose obviously broken, one ear torn, jaw hanging slackly which likely meant it, too, was broken. His shirt was ripped and blood-streaked flesh showed through the rent, also some mud and grit: sure signs he had been kicked repeatedly.

Hand on gun butt now, Cole rose from his knees on hearing a muffled cry. He saw scuffling figures down by the harness shed. A huge man was beating up on Careful Carmody. The freighter's legs would no longer hold him but he was supported between two men, all three jarring as Quinlan hammered his big fists into the already unconscious man. As Cole ran forward, they released Carmody and Quinlan glanced over his shoulder, snapped at the two hardcases,

'Take care of him.'

Then he proceeded to kick and stomp the downed freighter. Cole slowed, not believing his eyes for a moment. Then the two hardcases rushed him. He was in no mood for fair play here. He drew his gun — later the men swore they never even saw his right arm move — and fired twice. Both men fell, wounded through the upper legs, writhing and moaning in bloody agony.

The shots brought Quinlan spinning, and for a large man he moved mighty fast. He was breathing hard as he lifted his Colt and Cole stepped in, slammed his own gun down across the man's thick wrist. The six-gun fell and Quinlan grunted, grabbing at his wrist, but he curled thick lips and spat at Cole.

Next instant, Quinlan's vast bulk was slammed up against the shed hard enough to rattle the planks. Some harness on nails inside was jarred loose and fell, jingling.

Then Cole's smoking gun barrel moved in a blur, slamming from side to side, half a dozen times in the blink of an eye. The foresight ripped up Quinlan's face and his thick legs started to fold under him. Blood streaked across his cheeks, his nose lay over to one side, spurting thick streams of blood, one eyebrow was torn loose and his lips were cut from broken teeth. Cole lifted a knee into his crotch and Quinlan fell forward, hitting the ground in a huddled ball, barely conscious. Cole gave him one savage kick, then holstered his gun and knelt beside the bloody, disfigured Carmody.

The freighter was in terrible shape

with many broken bones and for a moment there Cole almost put a bullet into Quinlan. But he figured the big man had been marked for life. The word would soon spread about how he had come by such a marked-up face. (Quinlan grew a beard to hide the scars, later on. Though his inner scars were burning for revenge.)

★   ★   ★

'Maybe I should've killed him,' Cole murmured now as he rode towards his rendezvous with the ransom money. 'He's gonna do his best to kill me some day.'

But even though Quinlan was badly hurt, his wounds and their aftermath were nowhere near as bad as those inflicted upon Careful Carmody. The freighter would never be the same again, spoke vaguely, didn't recognize many of his old friends these days, could only get around on crutches.

Cole had heard several times that

Quinlan had vowed Cole would need a wheelchair when they had their inevitable reckoning. But, strangely, Devlin wouldn't allow Quinlan to go after Cole.

'The man's a lawman now, duly sworn and with Denver's approval. Kill him and we'll have marshals coming out of the woodwork, poking their noses into our affairs where we don't want 'em. Leave him be for now. We'll find a way to fix the sonuver when we're good and ready.'

Now, suddenly, Cole wondered for one fleeting moment, if maybe they had found that way — getting him out here alone, carrying twenty thousand dollars.

10

Reception

The ransom was to be paid at Birdwing Wells, but Larry Creed had inferred the boy was still being held in the crooked canyon near the Church Spire rock.

The places were miles apart and the fact that the ransom was to be paid over in the middle of the night — well, it seemed mighty suspect to Cole.

It smelled of a set-up. And if that was what it was, Quinlan was bound to be involved.

But there had been nothing in any of the ransom notes naming Cole as the one to deliver the ransom money. Linus had asked him as a personal favour; in any case, Cole felt it was his bounden duty to take on the job: he still felt responsible for Donny Charlton's abduction.

They couldn't have known ahead of time that he would be the one to make the delivery; in fact, there was a good chance they still didn't know *who* was bringing the money.

He couldn't work it out satisfactorily; maybe they planned to kill *whoever* brought the ransom. That way they would avoid being recognized or tied in with the kidnapping. They would realize that there would be a hue and cry afterwards. Bess Charlton would see to that, even if Linus didn't.

That was if they didn't kill the kid anyway, which was the only really safe way for kidnappers. Remove *all* chance of identification, starting with the abducted person, and whoever paid over the ransom, just to be sure.

He wasn't about to risk his neck by riding in blindly, following the instructions in the note to the letter. There was no room for improvisation or changes of direction: *right after moonset, leave the money under the round rock with one side sheared off, north side of the wells.*

That meant being in a certain place, at a certain time, close enough to reach the deposit rock by deadline.

A perfect plan for dry-gulching. They would know where he was at any given time after he passed the point that would allow him to reach the rock right after moonset.

Like hell!

It was late afternoon when he rode close to the hills, using the creeping shadows to make him hard to see. He had deliberately chosen the black mount and a dark-coloured packhorse so they would be hard to distinguish at night or in deep shadows around sundown. He wore dark clothing for the same reason.

He had brought a map with him, although he had been out here once before, looking for a horse-thief; he'd found him in a ravine, dead, the equally dead horse lying on top of him at the base of a cliff. It was dangerous country and Cole figured to get within a frog's leap of the Birdwing Wells while there was still light enough to see.

Which meant that anyone holed up with a rifle would be able to see him coming, too. But there was no avoiding it. He had studied the map closely and worked out a trail that would give him reasonable cover. Not that that meant much: if they were going to dry-gulch him, they would have all approaches under surveillance.

But, with the few facts he had, it was the best he could do. He rode with his rifle unsheathed, the butt resting on his right thigh; they would expect him to take precautions, so would shoot first, without warning.

This was country with lots of broken rock, crags jutting and hanging, making good lookouts for anyone wanting to see who was riding below, yet keeping hidden.

There were lots of shadows, deep black against the pale rock, but, at this time, there were still patches of sunlight that he was unable to avoid. His flesh crawled when he crossed these, eyes raking the heights, finger on the rifle trigger. He tensed at a flickering movement up there, relaxed almost immediately when he realized it was only a baby eagle, not yet ready to fly, flapping in a stick nest. While he watched the bird's antics, looking out for the homing mother with food, he caught another movement out of the corner of his left eye. It was on a neighbouring jutting crag, some twenty feet down from the rim.

That was no bird. It was a man changing position, likely growing cramped on the narrow ledge. A slanting shaft of sunlight flashed back at him from a rifle barrel.

Cole turned the black and the packhorse under a ledge and dismounted. He crouched in front of the big horse, certain he had not been seen by the watcher. The man was in the right place for an ambush, having a good view of the trail where it came out of a narrow, winding section. But he wouldn't be able to see the rider *in* that section, only when he reached the end and appeared in the open below the ledge.

He called up a picture of his map in his mind, relating the position of the ledge to where he knew Birdwing Wells lay ahead. Glancing at the sky, he smiled thinly: yeah! The sun was behind the hills now, throwing sawtoothed shadows in long, distorted patterns, misty rays fanning above the crags.

They would expect him to appear here just after sundown. That would still give him time to make his way carefully through the high ranges to the wells — where he could hole up until the moon set, and be ready to look for the broken rock and leave the ransom.

He figured he wasn't meant to ride out again.

But he had a plan to change that.

The first thing he did was hide the ransom in the bottom of a crevice, covering it with smaller rocks. The brown packhorse was docile, obedient, long used to obeying commands of men. Cole off-loaded the packs, took out his bedroll, and searched for and found a reasonably straight branch about three feet long, fallen from a tree that had long ago been struck by lightning. It was still strong and he broke off some of the thin, projecting branches, rammed the remaining shaft through his bedroll, end to end. He stood this vertically on his saddle, tied it in place with his lariat to saddle-horn and cantle. It was unsteady but would suffice. He hung a threadbare denim jacket over the top and jammed his hat on to hold it in place.

It would never pass in daylight, but in the shadows of a winding narrow trail through these hills it would look enough like a man to hold a watcher's attention. He hoped that the packhorse, once started, would automatically keep going, following the winding trail. He gave it a handful of oats, scratched it behind one ear. It nuzzled him and he stroked the muzzle, then stepped to the rear, slapping a hand across the rump.

The horse snorted a little but jerked forward and started along the deeply shadowed trail.

He glanced up between the towering walls and through the jagged slit they made against the darkening sky, saw the first faint stars. The three-quarter moon that had been hanging above the range all day began to glow as the light faded, fast now.

Hatless, he mounted, rifle in hand, and turned the black around, riding out of the broken entrance. He put the horse parallel with the rising hills, moving roughly in the same direction as the packhorse with its strange rig — and hoping it would hold and not topple from the saddle.

There was more light here and he was able to travel faster, but kept the black on softer ground where he could. He had worked out from his map where he should dismount and go in on foot, had climbed up a high rock for a better view and noted a lone pine tree about level with the position where he had seen the rifleman.

When he reached the tree he dismounted and tied the black to the trunk. He made a last check of his six-gun and rifle magazine, put a handful of spare shells in his shirt pocket, and ran back to the first slope of the hills. He began to make his way up. His game leg took the strain all right, but he moved cautiously. Stars were twinkling brightly above now. The moon was like a lantern washing the slopes with pale light — just enough to throw shadows over the twisting trail travelled by the packhorse. Sweat prickled him as the slope steepened and in two places he had to slide the rifle barrel through his belt at the back and use both hands to climb. He was breathing hard, trying not to snort too loudly.

His heart thudded against his ribs when he reached the place he had estimated would be level with the dry-gulcher's position. He paused, heaving deep breaths, steadying him-self, then, after quietly levering a shell into the breech, he clambered over the rock.

He had guessed well. There was the ledge below and to his right, with the man stretched out, his upper body rising a little so he could better see down to where the narrow trail opened onto the sandy area below.

The ambusher settled back, brought his rifle up to his shoulder. Cole heard the lever work, then, in the silence, the clip-clop of the slowly moving pack-horse below.

Cole eased forward, swore softly as the movement sent a handful of gravel spilling over the edge. It pattered across the legs of the man below and he spun onto his back. Cole dropped. There was a startled curse from the rifleman as he tried to roll aside and at the same time bring his gun around. The brass butt plate scraped across the ground. He almost had the weapon in position to shoot when Cole's body landed beside him. Cole threw himself across the man, jamming the hand holding the Winchester against a rock. He slammed it hard and the gun clattered. The man drew up his knees and kicked at Cole's belly.

One boot took him on the hip — the wounded one — and searing pain drove through him. Fuelled by the agony, he smashed his forehead into the other's face, felt nose and lips mash. Cole reared to his knees and slammed the rifle butt savagely across the ambusher's head. The body beneath him went limp.

Cole sat back, gasping, massaging his throbbing hip, hoping the rest of the reception committee weren't close enough to have heard the scuffle.

* * *

When the thwarted bushwhacker came round, he found he was bound hand and foot and his own neckerchief had been wadded up and pushed into his mouth to gag him.

He could hardly breathe through his nose: it was clogged with blood, but there was something hard blocking his left nostril as well. It hurt when he twitched his nose and he looked up with wide, puzzled eyes at Cole sitting on a nearby rock.

There was enough light for them to make out each other's features and Cole leaned forward, fumbled a match out of his shirt pocket. He held it up in front of the now thoroughly scared prisoner, thumbnail against the matchhead, ready to snap it into flame.

'Just gonna say this once, *amigo*. What you've got stuck up your nostril is a bunch of four vestas, just like this one. I flick my thumbnail and it lights up. I move it closer to its pards hanging out of your nose and . . . ' He stopped speaking, shrugged. 'You're dumb but I reckon you got enough brains to figure out what'll happen. And you can see why I'll only ask you just once what I want to know. You won't have a second chance. OK?'

The man was grunting endlessly, trying to speak, squirming in terror.

'Take it easy. What I'm gonna ask you is how many of your pards are waiting at Birdwing? When I ask, you nod if you're gonna tell me and I'll take that as your word you won't make a noise. If you break your word . . . '

The man was nodding frantically, bulging eyes fixed on the match only inches from his face: he understood all too well.

'OK. Consider the question asked. Now, do I light this or . . . Ah! You want to talk? Uh-huh. Now make sure you savvy what I want you to do . . . ' More frantic nodding and whining sounds. 'Here we go, then.'

Still holding the threatening vesta close to the battered face, Cole tore the wadded, saliva-wet kerchief from the man's mouth. The prisoner coughed and gagged, spat.

'I'm waiting!' Cole said impatiently.

'Thr . . . three. Quinlan insisted — on — comin' his — hisself.'

'Quinlan! So, that snake *is* behind it. All right, friend. One more question: have they got the kid with them?'

Panic-stricken eyes stared and Cole sighed, lifted his thumb, ready for the thumbnail strike against the match. Sweat struck his face as the prisoner quickly shook his head.

'No!'

'Not so damn loud! Where is he?'

'In — in some canyon Creed found earlier.'

'OK, friend. I know where it is.'

'What — what you gonna do with me?'

Cole put his vesta back in his pocket and reached for the ones still jammed in the man's nostril. Suddenly, with the immediate threat gone, the man stupidly lunged at Cole, hands and feet bound, trying to ram the top of his head into Cole's face, using his weight in an attempt to knock him over the ledge.

The sheriff dodged to one side, slipped and sprawled. There was a brief yell and a clatter of falling rocks as the bound man hurtled off the ledge. He crashed head first down to the clear area below where the packhorse waited patiently, its fake 'rider' having slid all over to one side, and was now minus the hat.

Cole looked down, but his prisoner wasn't moving: his head was twisted at an odd angle, a spreading stain darkening the shale underneath.

Well, that solved one problem, anyway,

11

Church Spire Rock

It was deathly quiet at Birdwing Wells. Not even a single insect buzzed or hummed or whined.

The moon was low down, sliding behind the bulk of the mountain, balancing on the crest briefly, then dropping gradually until it was hidden from sight. The glow still outlined the crest but slowly faded and a solid darkness claimed the slopes. The stars blazed coldly and shed a meagre light, but nothing could be seen to move.

Then there was a sound: a slight rasping of cloth as someone hidden in the rocks facing the north side of the wells changed position.

'Sit still, damn you!' hissed a deep voice and there was discernible anger in the few words.

'I hear him!' another voice said in hushed tones.

And then came the soft, cautious *plop* of a horse making its way to the water where the stars were reflected.

'He's not s'posed to — '

'*Christ!*' growled Quinlan in exasperation. His rifle came up as he glimpsed the shadowy outline of the rider on the slow-moving horse below.

The Winchester's crashing shots tore the night apart, slammed back from the rising rock walls, the sound intensifying as the other guns blazed.

The rider below was blown out of the saddle as the horse whinnied and reared, jerking away. It ran, dragging the body for several yards before it fell completely clear.

'Stop the goddamn hoss! It'll be carrying the ransom!'

Two rifles hammered and the horse whickered, reared, stumbled, and then slid down the slope to come to rest at the edge of the water, which rippled violently, shattering the stars' reflections.

Three men slid and lurched their way down the slope, all making for the fallen horse.

'Check Cole!' Quinlan snapped at one man who swore under his breath as he veered away and crossed to where the rider was sprawled face down.

Quinlan and the third man came upon the horse which was quivering its last. At a sign from Quinlan the other man began searching for the saddlebags which were jammed underneath.

The man upslope ripped out an oath. Quinlan spun. 'What . . . ?'

'This ain't Cole. It's Smitty! Looks like he fell off a cliff.'

Quinlan's huge bulk climbed up the slope and he looked down at the battered body of the man who had been left to cover the trail to the wells — and to cut off Cole's retreat.

'Son of a *bitch!*' Quinlan's deep voice thundered across Birdwing Wells. 'He killed Smitty and roped him to the saddle! Now, where the hell is he?'

'Gone after the kid, I reckon. Smitty

never did have much guts. He'd talk if Cole went to work on him.'

The man examining the empty saddlebags stood up and put in his two cents' worth:

'He'll have a damn good start! All the time we been waitin', thinkin' it was him comin' along that narrow trail — '

'Go get the horses!' growled Quinlan, at the same time cursing. He had been the one who insisted they leave the mounts at least half a mile away in a small wash, blocked off with brush, in case the animals sensed the lone rider's mount approaching the wells and whinnied, giving away their presence.

Now they would lose more time collecting the damn horses! And every minute, Cole was moving away from them — closing in on the Church Spire canyon where two more men had the kid.

'He won't get past Rooster or Blackie, Quick,' said the man who had examined the body, trying to sound reassuring.

'He better not,' gritted Quinlan, kicking the ground in his frustration. *'Now get the goddamn horses!'*

* * *

Cole was sorry he had had to sacrifice the packhorse — it had been obedient and uncomplaining — but it was necessary. He'd recovered his bedroll and replaced it with the dead man from up on the ledge, roping him in the saddle.

At best it was only a delaying action, but every minute he could confound Quinlan and whoever was with him was a bonus.

He knew the way to Church Spire Rock and even in the now moonless night he rode at a good clip. The black was strong and fast, actually ready to run a lot faster than Cole was allowing it to, but he was leery of the horse's strength. Some of these big, muscular stallions and geldings once they cut loose took a lot of stopping.

He was careful to keep the spur rowels away from the black and when he came out of the tangle of gulches and hills where the Birdwings were, he put the mount across the grassy flats until they ran into dusty ground, then he slowed again. The horse was not pleased, turning its head and taking a half-hearted snap at his left leg.

'Yeah, I know. If you had the chance, you'd chomp me good. I savvy your frustration.'

The horse wanted to run again, eager for the exercise, but now was the time to go into those canyons at a wary pace. Starlight was not very helpful in there with the high walls and narrow passages. He found himself all tensed up, mouth dry, belly muscles hard, hand gripping the rifle until his bones ached.

He was over-confident at one stage, became lost and thought for a time it would be damned near daylight before he found a way out of the tangle of canyons and dead ends he had ridden into.

But he spooked a cougar feeding on a deer it had downed and the animal had taken off. A glimpse of it silhouetted against the stars told him it was a female, heavily pregnant, which probably explained its willingness to flee — even wild cats had a powerful mother-instinct to make sure no harm came to the babies.

But the cat had shown him the way out of the scrambled knot of gulches: minutes later, he saw the spired rock rearing against the stars. He was closer than he had expected and now he dismounted and led the black by the reins up the first slopes of the mountain that hid the crooked, winding canyon Larry Creed had spoken of. Surprisingly, the black came willingly and it was not difficult to lead it through scattered rocks so that its hoofs did not disturb them.

When he reached the top and the downslope fell away into the start of the canyon, Cole pushed the rifle back into the saddle scabbard, punched in the top of his hat and filled it with water from his canteen. The black slurped it up, then Cole took the sawn-off shot-gun from the left hand saddlebag and a handful of shells from his pocket. He broke the gun and thumbed home two loads, but did not close the action fully: there was no safety and this was the only way he could make sure the gun wouldn't accidentally discharge if he stumbled or fell.

It was a long, snaking canyon and he had no idea where Creed's pards had holed up. It was a safe bet that it would be somewhere high on the slopes, so they could keep an eye on the approaches. This meant he had to travel slowly and watch both sides, hoping for some sign of a camp, but he figured they would have it well hidden.

The horse was growing restless now, had rested enough and was eager to be running again, cutting an exhilarating passage through the wind. The hoofs clattered a couple of times, freezing Cole in his tracks, ears straining.

The black was beginning to assert itself now, tugged at the reins, almost pulling him off balance. He stumbled, just managed to hold his tight grip on the shotgun, cursed the big animal.

'Damn you! I should've run you till you couldn't stand! Now, behave, goddammit!'

His efforts were puny against the strength of the horse, which was enjoying itself now, straining back with arched neck, keeping the reins taut so Cole couldn't get any slack, the leather starting to slide inexorably through his hands.

He suddenly let go and the horse stumbled, forefeet crossing as it tried to find solid footing after the unexpected release of pressure. In a flash, Cole was in the saddle, had the reins taut, throwing his weight back, the bit hard against the back of the black's mouth. Surprisingly, it accommodated his movements, settled, standing four-square solid now, head up, as if eagerly awaiting Cole's command.

He almost made the mistake of touching the spurs to the sweating flanks. But he stopped in time, settled the shotgun across his legs and flicked the reins.

'You're a playful devil, ain't you? Just like to let me know who's really in charge. OK, we go up, at an angle towards that . . . ' Cole stood in the stirrups, staring unbelievingly.

There was a red spark up there, this side of the crest, at least twenty feet below. *A red spark* — that could only be coals of a banked campfire, or one that hadn't been fully extinguished earlier. The black's antics had occurred over a considerable area of ground, taken them more than halfway through the winding canyon.

That had to be Creed's cronies' camp, maybe outside a cave or overhang of rock. He couldn't risk the black's deciding to put on another demonstration of its independence, so he ground-hitched the horse. He could see the animal wasn't pleased.

'You stay put and be ready to carry me, and, hopefully, a young boy not more'n forty-fifty pounds . . .'

He patted the muzzle and almost had his hand bitten. He smiled ruefully and started up the slope. It was awkward carrying the shotgun, but he had figured it for the best weapon to use in the confines of the canyons.

The slope was steeper than it looked and he had to make his progress in a series of slow zigzags across. His breath burned the back of his throat with his efforts and the wounded leg was acting up, aching, not as strong as it had been originally. It gave way unexpectedly and, leaning forward, he had to put down a hand to keep from falling.

It saved his life.

A rifle crashed not five yards above and he heard the ripping sounds of the bullets passing over his back. He dropped and rolled now, snapping the shotgun closed, coming over onto his belly. The gun flashed above him again and the bullet kicked stones and dirt against his side.

Then the shotgun thundered and he glimpsed the dark shape of the guard up there, doubled over as if kicked in the belly by a cranky mustang. The man gave a strangled croak and fell forward, rolling part-way down the slope.

'Rooster!' someone called from a deeper black patch above the coals of the campfire, which he could see now. 'Who the hell is that?'

If the man expected an answer he was disappointed. Cole could make out the entrance to a cave now and the man lurched out, rifle butt braced against his hip, lever working as he fired again and again, raking the slope.

Cole spun away to one side and while still on his left side, triggered the shotgun's second barrel. The gunman staggered as if he had hit a wall, but he wasn't about to give up.

He took a couple more steps, getting off two wild shots, the last one pointing to the ground. Cole dropped the shotgun, palmed up his Colt and fired once.

The man fell, rolling and sliding down past Cole, the rifle clattering after him.

Cole ignored him, started up the slope, hoping there *had* been only two guards. Crouching by the cave entrance, he called warily,

'Donny? Donny? You in there?'

No answer, but someone coughed deep inside the cave.

'It's Sheriff Cole, Donny. Are you OK?'

'I — I'm OK, Sher'ff,' called a shaky, thin voice from back in the darkness. 'Only — I ain't Donny. I'm Sam Bale.'

12

Home on the Range

The kid was a mess. He was still wearing Donny Charlton's jacket but it was stained with mud and red rock dust, the seam was torn on one shoulder and a pocket was starting to break away.

He had a black eye and his face was smeared with dirt. Large front teeth and freckles, a formless kid's nose and eyebrows that were barely discernible — this was Sammy Bale. His hair was tow-coloured like Donny's, but there must be at least another dozen boys of varying ages in town with the same colour hair.

Cole could see how simple it would be for the kidnappers to make a mistake: likely they had been cowboys or hardcases hired for the abduction and not actually knowing Donny Charlton by sight; they would have been told to look for a tow-haired seven-year-old, probably wearing a reasonably new jacket if it was in the cool of evening near the start of the night-time fireworks' show.

Sammy Bale had a heavy cold; he was sniffling and coughing occasionally even as Cole cleaned him up and gave him some food, It was obvious from the way Sam ate that he hadn't been fed much lately.

'What happened, Sam?'

The boy swallowed the last of his fifth corn dodger, wiped the back of a wrist across his mouth and started to use the same wrist on his moist nostrils. Cole stopped him, gave him a kerchief. Sam blew into it and offered it back. Cole lifted a hand.

'Consider it a gift, Sam. Now tell me how come you were snatched instead of Donny?'

'I dunno. I mean, I fell in the river and Donny pulled me out and I was shiverin' with this cold an' he give me his new jacket to wear.' The boy's bright-blue eyes lit up. 'It's a beauty. I wish it was mine.'

'You ask Donny could you keep it on?'

'Sort of.' He hung his head a little, watching Cole's face from under his thin eyebrows. 'I — I said I was still cold and put on a bit of a wheeze or two. Donny said I could keep it on but I'd have to give it back when his ma showed up. She's kinda — snooty, Donny's ma, you know?'

'Haven't had much to do with her but I got that impression.'

Sam gave a quick smile, glad to have Cole agree with him. 'Anyway, we was scavengin' around for some spare rockets and these two fellers come up and said they had found three or four unfired ones. We started to go with 'em, but one grabbed Donny by the arm and lifted him clear off the ground, carried him off somewhere behind a wagon. I got scared and tried to run but I tripped and I hit my head.' He pulled his hair back and a bruise and slight swelling were still obvious. 'I was knocked out, I guess. When I come round I'm lyin' over this dark feller's lap on his hoss with my wrists tied behind my back. They brought me to this cave an' I been here ever since.'

'Know who the man was?'

'Rooster — the first one you killed. The other was Blackie someone.'

Cole rolled a cigarette, lit up and smoked thoughtfully. Sam started eating again.

'Not too much, too fast. If your belly's been starved for a few days, you go easy.'

Sam looked as if he would argue but then thought better of it, wiped his hands down the front of the stained jacket.

'Donny's ma'll throw a fit when she sees this.'

'Yeah, could be. I'm wondering what happened to Donny. Everyone's convinced he was the one kidnapped. And how come your ma didn't raise hell when you went missing?'

'Aw — I dunno.' Small shoulders shrugged; he didn't seem unduly worried that his mother hadn't reported him missing. He wouldn't meet Cole's gaze.

'You been running off from home now and again?' Cole asked suddenly and the way Sam jumped and moved a little away from him gave him his answer. 'You been skedaddling off for so long that your ma's gotten used to it, no longer bothers if you don't show up till you're good and ready. That it?'

Cole's voice had anger in it and the boy started to cringe, head on one side as if expecting a cuff. Cole immediately relented.

'Hey, boy, don't do that! I ain't gonna hit you. Is that why you run away every now and again? Because your ma whips you?'

'She don't, but he does sometimes when he's been at the likker.'

'Who's 'he'?'

Sam took his time answering, pulled some grass and tore up the blades one by one as he spoke, eyes downcast.

'Well, sir, my ma — she never been married, see?' He waited, challengingly, but Cole's face remained blank. 'My pa was killed before he could marry her and she said she never wanted no other man for a husband . . . '

'It's OK, Sam. I understand. She feels the need now and again for a man's company, is that it?'

Sam looked relieved and smiled briefly. 'I guess. But this feller, this Winston, says he's my uncle. He's been hangin' around, don't seem to wanna leave. I know Ma *wants* to get rid of him but he's sort of — taken over. She told me we'd run off if the farm wasn't all she had in the world, and she wants to keep it — for me.'

There was a hint of tears in the boy's eyes and voice now. He paused, gulping.

'Sam, your ma sounds like a good woman to me. But we've got to get outta here before some other men involved in your kidnapping turn up. And I've got to find Donny Charlton! You any idea where the hell he could be?'

Sam didn't and Cole figured it was time they were somewhere else. He stood, dropped the cigarette butt and crushed it.

'C'mon, kid. I'll take you home.'

* * *

'Where the hell is he goin'?' Red Carlin snapped irritably as Quinlan led the way down the dark slope. 'Would be better if the damn moon was still out.'

'Be a whole *lot* better if you kept your mouth shut!' Quinlan growled.

'We ain't gonna pick up any trail in the dark, Quick,' said the third man, Smoky Hill, trying to sound reasonable. No one wanted to stir Quinlan's temper; when the man was crazy mad he didn't differentiate between friend and foe.

'Where d'you think he's going?' Quinlan asked, his deep voice rasping. 'He's gonna take the kid back home, for Chrissakes.'

There was silence and, riding side by side, Red and Smoky exchanged a glance, or as much of one as each could see in the dark.

'Quick,' Red said, licking his lips. 'We heard his hoss while gettin' our own mounts, and it wasn't goin' back towards Barberry.'

'That's a fact, Quick,' added Smoky quietly.

Quinlan reined down, yanking the reins so hard his mount snorted and pranced in protest.

'Is that right? Well, he had to find his way outta the canyon, didn't he? It twists and turns like a snake with colic. *After* he clears it is where we'll pick up his proper trail. It ought to be light enough then, and it'll lead back to Barberry. Don't make sense any other way.'

Smoky and Red were silent, then

Smoky leaned out and nudged Red's leg, urging him by nods of his head to speak up. After a few moments he heard Red clear his throat.

'Quick, he could be makin' his way back to the Bale farm.' Quinlan snapped his head up and Red added, quickly, 'All along that kid reckoned he was Sammy Bale, not the Charlton brat.'

'Little swine was just actin' up ornery,' Quinlan said, harshly. '*D. Charlton* was sewed into the collar of the coat he was wearing. He was just trying to be smart so's we'd let him go.'

Red sighed, glanced at Smoky for some back-up but Hill remained quiet. Red swore softly; now he was left alone to argue with Quinlan and he didn't know too many men who'd won such a contest. Didn't know any! But he had spoken now and had to back up his reasoning.

'He had a good explanation for the coat, Quick. The Charlton kid lendin' it to him after he fell in the river, 'cause he had a cold — and you can't deny he sure does have a bad cold, snotty-nosed little hellion.'

'Red, I'm convinced we had Donny or Danny Charlton, whatever the hell his name is. But, as I said, it'll be light enough to read Cole's tracks soon. *Then* we decide which way we go. Now, that's it! Both of you shut up till we get outta these damn canyons!'

Red and Smoky were glad to obey.

★ ★ ★

Mattie Bale was in her late twenties, quite good-looking, though careworn from long years of hard work and worry about everyday living. The farm wasn't large but it was a lot of work for one woman, with only the occasional help of an active eight-year-old boy, when she could nail him down for long enough.

She had actually been glad when Winston Bale had turned up, brother of Steven, Sammy's father. He had been

193

obliging enough at first, pitching in, making the place more like a farm should be — and then he moved into her bed.

'I'd be your brother-in-law if Steve hadn't been killed and you know a man's brother can claim his rights from his sister-in-law when she's widowed.'

'That's not a law!' she argued. 'It's what some folk want to believe, is all.'

He was a handsome man, Winston. His smile had won him many a throbbing female heart since he was in his teens. He always had his way with women — always. And Mattie would be no different. 'Well, *I* believe it,' he told her, flashing that smile. 'I surely do.'

And, in the end, the smile worked for him once again.

★ ★ ★

But his original eagerness to work and build up the farm had its edge blunted soon after and he spent a lot of time lounging around the cabin, or fishing down at the creek. He was good to Sammy, took him fishing with him, but didn't care whether it was a school day or not and Sammy lost a deal of education. And he didn't mind boxing the boy's ears when Sam annoyed him in some way, either.

Mattie found she was working harder than ever now there were three of them — tending her vegetable patch, trapping rabbits and possums and squirrels and other small game just to put meat on the table. Once or twice Winston brought in a fish big enough to share, and one time he actually hunted down and killed a deer.

But mostly he did little around the farm and began to boss both Mattie and Sammy: 'Time to milk the cow, boy. Get it done.' 'Go collect some more eggs from the chicken pen Mattie, I fancy a big omelette for my lunch.' 'Go into town and bring me back some fresh tobacco — oh, and a bottle of Mannering's rye — he'll give you credit.'

'I *hate* going near that saloon,' Mattie complained and his dark eyes narrowed.

'You do what I say, woman! And tell Judd Reason I want to see him, too.'

She stiffened when he said that. 'Why d'you want to see that snide land dealer?'

'Why d'you just ask for a smack in the mouth by givin' me an argument! *You do what I say!*'

She knew what he was about: he was negotiating the sale of the farm, somehow going to fix it with Judd Reason, although the farm title was in her name. But Winston Bale had some way around that, and she knew she and Sammy wouldn't see any money from such a sale.

But it never came to that, for Winston devised a bigger plan to make him rich beyond his dreams, right after she arrived back from the Fourth of July hoedown in Barberry, and they found a frightened Donny Charlton hiding under the tarp in the rear of the buckboard.

'Who the hell's this? Where's Sammy?' Winston grabbed young Donny by his shirt and shook him, glaring at Mattie.

'I didn't know he was there, Winston! I swear!'

'Where the hell is Sammy?'

'I — I couldn't find him,' she explained, voice trembling. 'You know what he's like, always running off and hiding. I — I couldn't find Donny here, neither, to ask where Sam was. I thought they'd both run off together. You know Sam always comes back after a few days . . . '

Winston shook Donny. 'What're you doin' here, boy? Where's Sam?'

'They — they kidnapped, him. They thought he was me.'

Mattie and Winston stared, Mattie gasping.

'Two men — they jumped us, said they had some sky rockets for us. But one grabbed Sam and t'other dragged me off and cuffed me hard — said I was to keep my mouth shut or some night he'd come an' slit my throat. He showed me his knife an' everything. He thought I was Sammy. I was scared and hid under the tarp in your buckboard, but I din' know it was yours, Mrs Bale, honest Injun . . . '

'That's all right, Donny, it's all right. But what've they done with my Sammy?'

'I — I heard 'em say whoever they worked for was gonna ask for a big ransom, ten or twenty thousand dollars. Said Linus would pay it for me, that he'd be able to raise the money easy, him being with the bank.'

Winston leaned down quickly, holding Donny's shoulder hard so that the boy squirmed. 'Twenty thousand! For the likes of you! I don't believe it!'

'It's true!' Donny was upset now, tears brimming in hsi eyes. 'I — I want to go home to my ma. Those men scared me . . . '

'That's all right, Donny. I'll drive you home. But we'll have some food first and — '

'The kid stays here,' Winston cut in, smiling crookedly, holding the boy's arm in a crushing grip. 'I mean, he's what you call a valuable asset, ain't you, kid? I bet they don't care who they pay that ransom to, long as they get you back safe and sound. Hell, I ain't greedy! I'll even settle for a nice big fat re-ward for keepin' this young man safe. 'Course it might be a few days before I let 'em know we've got him. By then, they'll be glad to pay just about anythin' I ask!'

He winked at the shocked, white-faced Mattie.

'Now, don't say your brother-in-law ain't got a brain or two in his head, eh?'

'Does your brain tell you what happens to Sam when they find out he's not the one they thought?' Her voice trembled and she began to shake. 'They'll probably kill him so he can't identify them!'

Winston composed his face. 'Don't reckon they will. Anyway, this one stays put. I ain't gonna let him outta my sight till I decide to tell that banker where I got him — an' how much it's gonna cost to get him back!'

13

The Ransom

Red Carlin looked smug when they found the tracks some distance from the entrance to the snakelike canyon. They pointed towards the distant Bale farm, a long journey through the hills and the plains beyond.

'Reckon the kid was young Sam Bale after all.'

Smoky sucked down a sharp breath; he couldn't believe Red could be so loco as to rub Quinlan's nose in it this way.

The big man, squatting beside the tracks left by Cole, looked up bleakly, scratching idly at his short beard.

'Could be. Or Cole's got some idea of hiding the Charlton kid out there. Either way, we follow. And we do it without a lot of stupid talk.' He set his glare on Red, who swallowed and nodded, running the tip of his tongue around his thin lips.

'Whatever you say, Quick. I wouldn't put it past that damn sheriff to try to hide Donny Charlton.'

Quinlan straightened, hitched up the gun belt around his thick waist.

'Kid don't matter — to hell with him, whoever he is. I want Cole — we've got some squarin' away to do. But better'n that, he still has the ransom money. *That*'s what counts now.'

Both Red and Smoky Hill nodded gently; for a while there they had forgotten that the whole point of this was to collect the money, had been too busy trying to decide the identity of the kid.

Now, like Quinlan said, that didn't matter: it was the cash that counted.

The cash and Cole, Red corrected himself.

He sure as hell wouldn't want to be in that sheriff's shoes when Quinlan should finally catch up with him.

Sam Bale was riding up behind Cole on the big black. It was so wide in the body that his short legs were stretched out and he squirmed around a lot in discomfort.

'Stay still,' Cole said shortly.

'I feel like I'm doin' the splits. My belly an' legs're nearly in a straight line, this blamed jackass is so darn wide!'

Cole reined up and Sam slid off gratefully, rubbing his groins and hips, stamping his feet.

'That feels good. Think I might run alongside for a spell.'

'With your legs we'll be going backwards. C'mon, sit in front of me. I'll slide back a bit in the saddle.'

It was better but Sam held the saddle horn, pushing against it constantly to keep it from pressing into his belly. 'I'm gonna be dead before we get home!'

'You keep up that bitchin' and you might be. You been playing too long with Donny Charlton. Linus reckons he's always complaining about something.'

'Yeah, well maybe he has cause to, way Linus treats him.'

'The considered opinion of an eight-year-old, eh? They just don't get along, is all. Like you and me won't, you keep bellyaching. You think riding like this is worse than being in that cave?'

Sam went quiet. They covered another mile before he said in a quieter tone, 'I was scared they was gonna kill me.'

'Understandable. They seemed mean types.'

'*They* was scared of someone called Quinlan. Boy, he sure had that Rooster and Blackie buffaloed. Kept checkin' my ropes, one or t'other, sayin' to make *blamed* sure I couldn't get away or Quinlan'd kill 'em both.'

'Guess he wanted it to go off just right, seeing as the kidnapping was his idea in the first place.'

Sam twisted a little and craned his

neck to look up into Cole's dusty face.

'What gave you that notion?'

Cole tensed, frowning. After a few moments he said, 'Well, maybe he had some help from Brack Devlin. You know who he is?'

'I've heard of him. But no one mentioned his name while they had me.'

'Then why d'you doubt it was Quinlan's idea?'

'Just somethin' they said.'

'Which was?'

'Hey! Lookit! There's the farm!' Sam started squirming, throwing his short legs over the saddle horn and dropping off the black. 'Never thought I'd be so glad to see it!'

'Come back here! It's a couple of miles yet over those hills . . . Sam! Ah, dammit!'

He set the black after the boy who ploughed into thick brush, dodging about so the black couldn't follow without Cole having to keep a tight rein, trying to find a clear passage. The boy being so small, he could crawl under the bushes and it was hard to see just where he was.

The little tyke had decided to have some fun, damnit!

Cole was still fighting the black — the horse not happy at being constantly scratched up by the stiff, prodding brush — when the laughing kid burst out way ahead and scooted up the slope like a young, gangling deer.

Swearing at being outwitted by an eight-year-old, Cole forgot the livery man's admonition about spurs.

He touched them to the black's flanks, aiming on driving it through the dense brush in as straight a line as possible.

Bam! The world seemed to explode around him. The black whickered and half-reared, then snorted, swung its head and bit his lower leg. Even with the leather of the half-boot between his flesh and those big teeth, it hurt like the devil. Cole yelled, automatically leaned down to rub his lower leg.

The black plunged away and the brush raked across Cole's shoulders, swept him from the saddle. Spiky brush tore at his clothes, ripped a line of red across one cheek, caught under his six-gun butt, flicking it from the holster.

Cole dived after it and by the time he recovered the Colt and stood up, angrily freeing his loose shirt from snagging brush, the horse was through and running free, mane and tail flying.

Above, on top of the hill, he heard the full-blooded chortling amusement of the boy, who waved cheekily.

'Hope you catch him — eventually!'

Then he turned and disappeared over the crest of the hill, just an echo of his tinkling laughter reaching the angry sheriff.

★   ★   ★

Mattie Bale felt the hard ground against her knees as she worked in the vegetable garden, some twenty yards away from the cabin. She grabbed a handful of her old skirt, bunching the cloth so it made a pad beneath her sore knees.

At the same time she lifted her head. Her face was shaded by her straw hat as she looked towards the entrance to the root cellar just past the south end of the garden.

She thought she heard Donny Charlton again. Her heart started to beat faster, and she flicked her gaze towards the house, but there was no sign of Winston. Which didn't mean he wasn't watching from behind the curtain in the window of the bedroom.

It wasn't right, keeping Donny here! Especially locked away in the root cellar. But Winston Bale had his mind set on claiming the ransom for himself, or at least a substantial reward in exchange for Donny.

She had thought of trying to sneak out at night to release the boy, but Winston locked the bedroom door and kept the key on a thong around his neck.

And he always had an arm thrown across her body so that she only had to stir or turn over and he was instantly awake.

Funny! That cry wasn't coming from the root cellar — it was much clearer than Donny's muffled calls.

She heard it again and straightened, standing up completely now, turning to look at the low hogback rise. Her breath caught in the back of her throat as she glimpsed the small figure hurtling down the slope, tow hair wild, waving, the piping voice calling her name.

'Oh, dear God! Thank you, thank you!' She waved and hiked up her skirts, starting to run towards Sammy as his short legs pumped frantically in his excitement and pleasure at being home again.

Then she came to an abrupt halt, panting, alarmed to see a rider on a big black horse coming over the crest. He bore down on the running boy who looked wildly over his shoulder. The rider leaned down, fisted up a handful of Sammy's jacket and lifted him bodily, depositing the boy in front of him on the horse.

She put a hand to her mouth, screaming for Winston — of *all people!* But the rider continued on at a more sedate pace, rode into the yard and dropped Sammy to the ground only a few yards away.

The boy ran to his mother, who picked him up and was almost choked by the thin arms clamping around her head and neck. She felt her heart melt, the sting of tears.

'My! I haven't had *that* big a welcome for years!'

'Get down from that hoss, mister! And careful!'

Winston came around a corner of the cabin, holding a rifle, covering Cole, paying no attention to Sammy or the woman. The sheriff dismounted slowly, watching Winston closely.

'Who the hell's this?' Bale demanded.

'That's Sheriff Cole from Barberry,' Mattie told her brother-in-law. 'We've never met, but I know him by sight.'

Cole touched a hand to his hatbrim. 'Pleased to meet you, ma'am. You don't need that rifle, mister.'

'I'll decide that.'

'For heaven's sake, Winston! He's a *lawman!*'

'The sheriff rescued me from the kidnappers, Ma. Shot 'em both. *Wow!* Is he fast!'

Winston suddenly looked uncertain and the rifle barrel sagged. 'You ain't gonna harm the boy?'

Cole flicked his bleak gaze across the man and settled it on Mattie. 'Your boy was kidnapped in mistake for Donny Charlton, ma'am . . .'

'Oh, yes, I know. Donny told us . . .'

'Shut up, Mattie!'

But it was too late and Cole studied Winston as the woman explained how Donny had turned up here, some days ago, terrified the kidnappers were going to come after him.

'Where is he now?'

Mattie glanced at Winston who

forced a weak smile. 'Well, the kid's so scared I put him in the root cellar. Convinced him he'd be safe there, no one could harm him.'

'How long's he been in there?'

'We-ell — '

'Ever since he arrived!' Mattie said quickly, cutting in over Winston's halting explanation; she saw how she could finally get rid of the man and his threat to her and Sam. 'Winston has some idea he'll hold him, and collect the ransom himself!'

'Damn you, woman!'

Winston brought up the rifle quickly but there was a gunshot and the weapon was smashed from his hands. He jumped back, hands tingling, looking at the splintered rifle stock on the ground at his feet.

Mattie cringed, hugging Sam tightly to her, staring wide-eyed at the smoking Colt in the sheriff's hand. He started forward and Winston, half-crouching, backed away.

'Listen. I din' mean no harm! It — it

just seemed that if someone was willin'
to pay for the kid's return — '

Cole hit him in the mouth, a
backhanded blow from the left. Winston
staggered and dropped to one knee.

'Sam, you go let Donny out.' Cole,
keeping an eye on Winston, fumbled
open one saddlebag on the sweating
black and took out a set of manacles.

Winston was on his feet when Cole
walked up to him and told him to hold
out his hands.

'What the hell're you doin'? Aagh!
Judas, they're too tight! You've pinched
my skin!'

'You're lucky I don't break your jaw!
What kind of snake are you, locking up
a kid scared out of his wits in a dark
cellar!' Cole shoved Winston roughly.
'Get over there and sit under that tree.
You move and I'll shoot you in the leg.'

'Wh — what you gonna do with me?'

'Take you back to Barberry and up
before Judge Cannon. He's got a
grandson about Donny Charlton's age.
I reckon you'll be either working on the

chain gang or spending the next couple of years in the territorial pen.'

'What? For keepin' a kid safe in a root cellar?'

'Sammy told me about you taking over this farm and aiming to sell it out from under Miz Bale. And I got a good memory for faces. Yours is on a dodger from Creek County, in connection with a Wells Fargo robbery. 'Winn Bailey'. Know that name?'

Winston's shoulders slumped. Mattie frowned.

'Is that true, Sheriff? That he's a wanted man?'

'Yes, ma'am. I reckon he was hiding out here on your farm, it being so isolated. Saw a chance to make himself some easy money.'

Mattie walked across and slapped Winston's face. 'I don't see how you can possibly be Steven's brother! He was a fine man — '

'Yeah, yeah — and a poor one,' Winston said, surly now. ''Honest Steve' we used to call him at Wells

Fargo. Needed some extra money so's he could marry you, make an honest woman of you, and took a job as shotgun guard. Only he picked a stage that was held up and like the fool he was, died tryin' to stop the robbers. When I ran into a little trouble myself an' we had to scatter I recollected him talkin' about you and this farm he was buyin' . . . '

Mattie, fighting back tears, looked as if she would like to spit upon him. Then Sammy came running back with a filthy-looking Donny Charlton. The boy was blinking in the sunlight.

'Oh, you poor soul! Come on up to the house and I'll give you a good wash. Sam's clothes should fit you . . . '

She led the subdued Donny towards the cabin. Sam started after her but Cole called him back.

'Sam. You were going to tell me something when you got all excited about seeing your farm and ran off.'

The boy blinked up at the tall sheriff. 'I wasn't gonna tell you anythin'.'

'You were talking about Rooster or Blackie saying something about who set up Donny Charlton's kidnapping.'

'Aw, yeah.' Sam glanced towards the cabin where his mother and Donny had now disappeared. 'Er — maybe I got it wrong. Might be better I don't say nothin' an' get someone into trouble.'

Cole leaned down, making his face stern. 'How about *you* being the one to get into trouble by *not* telling me?'

The sheriff flicked his gaze towards the sullen Winston in manacles slumped under the tree. Sam drew down a sharp breath.

'We-ell. They was talkin' about the ransom and how much it was, twenty thousand. Blackie said he couldn't imagine bein' so rich, that someone could lose that much gamblin'. And Rooster said, well, he reckoned it was a right smart idea of the banker's to have his own stepson kidnapped and then pay off his gamblin' debts with a ransom put up by the kid's mother — '

' 'The banker'? Linus Charlton?'

Sammy Bale shrugged. 'Guess so. Dunno who else they could mean.'

'No,' Cole said slowly. 'Me neither.'

14

All Squared Away

Cole knew Quinlan and his men would be coming after him and Sammy Bale.

'Miz Bale . . . '

'Mattie, please, Sheriff.'

He nodded. 'I answer best to just 'Cole'. Mattie, there are some men after me. The ones who kidnapped Sam. I reckon they'll be here soon and I don't want you left to face 'em. The leader's a miserable snake, goes by the name of Quinlan, and if he finds he's missed me here, he's likely to get real mad, might even burn the farm.'

'Oh, no!' Her hand went to her throat.

'It's possible, so I figure you and the boys, and Winston, better come with me to Barberry.'

'What if we meet this Quinlan along the way?'

'There'll be a fight. I won't lie to you. But it'll be best out in the open.'

Her teeth tugged at her bottom lip and then she nodded. 'All right. If you can hitch up the buckboard, I'll get ready and find some decent clothes for Donny to wear. I suppose I should try to repair his jacket, too. I don't know Mrs Charlton, but I hear she's kind of — finicky.'

He smiled. 'That's one word for it.'

Winston was still manacled under the tree and he watched as Cole prepared the buckboard.

'I can ride if you put my hands in front.'

The sheriff merely looked at him, finished harnessing the team.

'I won't try to escape. Give you my word.'

'You'll ride in the back of the buckboard,' Cole told him flatly.

And that was how they left the farm a short time later. Cole watched the backtrail frequently. Winston was stretched out on a tarp in the back of the buckboard, the boys riding up front with Mattie Bale who handled the team expertly.

Cole rode to high ground where he could, searching for sign of Quinlan, and it wasn't long before he saw a dust cloud that brought him standing up in the stirrups. It was coming in from the right direction, maybe slightly north, but by now Quinlan would have seen *their* dust and swung around to follow and check it out.

Cole rode back to the buckboard, coming up on the driving side. Mattie read his face, stiffened, and looked past him. She sucked in a sharp breath.

'Are those the men?'

''Fraid so, Mattie. We left it a mite late. The boys better get in the back, you too. You can handle the reins from the tray if you crouch down.'

'Yes, I've done it before.' At his quizzical glance she smiled. 'I grew up in Comanche country, in a sod hut. *Several* sod huts. We had to abandon them from time to time and twice I recall we had to outrun renegade bucks.'

'Don't want a job as deputy, do you?'

She laughed and slowed the team while the boys clambered into the back. Then she handed the reins to Sam while she followed. She knelt down, the reins running over the back of the driving seat now as she experimented to make sure she could give the signals to the team smoothly.

Winston huddled down lower; he was a man who always looked out for Number One. The boys were excited and just a little afraid. Neither wanted to show fear in front of the other, but their smiles were fixed.

Guns started banging. Just faint whipcracks at first, the bullets puffing dust well behind the buckboard. Cole unsheathed his Winchester but didn't return fire yet; he had no ammunition to waste.

Quinlan was unmistakable with his huge bulk, forking a big palomino, the rifle like a toy in his hands. Red Carlin rode a few yards to Quinlan's left, while Smoky Hill was at about the same distance to the right.

Cole could guess Quinlan's strategy: they would fire into the buckboard from the three different positions, likely trying for the team. Just downing one horse would be enough to wreck the buckboard — and, of course, they figured Cole would haul rein and ride back to help.

Then *he* would be the target for the three rifles.

So Cole angled away from the buckboard, trying to draw Quinlan's fire, but the big man made no attempt to go after him or even direct the guns towards the sheriff.

'You son of a bitch!' Cole murmured, swinging back towards the racing vehicle. 'Make targets out of women and kids!'

Quinlan knew Cole, knew the man wouldn't abandon the woman and boys, and also wouldn't want them harmed. Quinlan and his men were closing in on the vehicle now and splinters flew from the sides. Winston yelled. The boys lay flat, trying to press their small bodies into the rough planks. Mattie stretched out, driving more or less blindly now, but if she stayed on her knees, she would be too easy a target.

She guessed Quinlan would use her to draw Cole into his trap. There was little she could do about it, and she was worried the boys were in danger from the flying lead. Winston could take his chances, but the boys' safety concerned her.

Cole took the reins in his teeth, threw the rifle to his shoulder and quickly beaded Red Carlin, the closest rider. The gun jumped as he squeezed off his shot and a moment later, Red tumbled from the saddle.

In that brief passage of time Quinlan and Smoky Hill had closed in. Smoky was almost close enough now to leap from his saddle into the rear of the clattering, bouncing vehicle. He was poised to try and Cole, busy dodging bullets from Quinlan's rifle, couldn't get a bead on Hill. Then Sammy and Donny rose up and began throwing something at the killer. Smoky lifted his arms, dodging as well as he could, then three large potatoes and a cabbage hit him. He yelled as he tumbled out of the saddle. He bounced and screamed as he skidded in under the back wheels.

The buckboard bounced wildly and Mattie cried out as she was flung into Winston, almost losing her grip on the reins. He kicked at her but Sam had another cabbage in his fist now and slammed it down into Winston's face, screwing and pushing. The leaves tore loose, Winston started choking.

By then Mattie had control again.

Quinlan was too big and awkward to make the leap across but he bared his teeth, throwing a wild glance at the racing black with Cole lifting his rifle again, before aiming his own gun at the woman.

Cole drove home the spurs into the black's flanks.

In two mighty, whickering leaps the big horse smashed into Quinlan's palomino and both mounts went down, all a-tangle, throwing the riders.

Cole rolled maybe a dozen times, losing the rifle, digging in his boot heels in an attempt to slow his slide. Quinlan was rolling, too, but his large bulk didn't slide so far and he spun onto his side, teeth bared white against his jet-black beard, as he brought up his Colt.

He fired twice and stones leapt against Cole's face as he kicked away, spun and came up to one knee. Quinlan's six-gun swung around towards him, but it was Cole's Colt that blasted three fast shots. The lead knocked Quinlan flat but he tried to rise on his elbow, even though already choking on blood from a neck wound. He brought his gun up, holding it awkwardly in both his huge hands, eyes crazy and bulging with hate.

But the effort was just too much and he fell back, dead.

★   ★   ★

Linus Charlton knew something had gone wrong.

The ransom should have been paid over by now and young Donny returned. He didn't want any real harm to come to the boy but he couldn't help feeling pleased at the fright the kid would have had. He hoped Quinlan and the others hadn't been *too* tough with him.

But it was important that the ransom was paid over quickly — that was his masterstroke.

For weeks he had sweated and felt his ulcer burning holes in his stomach over the debt he owed Brack Devlin — via Mannering, curse his hide! If he had realized that Mannering at the Delta was part of Devlin's group he would never have turned a card or thrown a dice . . . *No — he would have, just the same.* When the gambling fever gripped him, he would have bet his own mother's wedding ring if there was just that slim chance of his luck turning . . .

He was lucky in one way, being president of the local bank, but in another it caused him more worry than he had ever known in his life before.

'We gave you all that credit, Linus, because you run the bank, you damn fool!' Mannering had told him.

As soon as the words were spoken, Linus felt sick and faint. 'The — the bank has nothing to do with it!'

'You think not? You think you have such a winnning personality — combined with a *losing streak* — that I would extend you all that credit? Wake up, Linus! You owe money, a lot of money, and you run the local bank. Doesn't that set ideas running around in that porridge you use for brains?'

He almost did faint then. 'No! It — it's ridiculous! I can't use the bank's money! It's — it's more than my job is worth.'

Mannering had looked at him bleakly. 'Wrong, Linus. It could be more than your *life* is worth.'

It was only a matter of time, of course. Pressure, relentless pressure — the threat of losing his house, his job, *Bess* — and he was driven into the hell of embezzlement.

Surprisingly, after the first time — and doing it successfully — it became easier. Twice more, and then the amount he had stolen from the bank reached 5,000 dollars.

He almost died of fright; it was such a large amount to account for that the first audit, due in a month or so, would pick it up almost immediately.

That was when Mannering informed him that he actually owed the money to Brack Devlin's group. A few days later Quick Quinlan arrived, and when he left Linus was nursing two broken fingers, with the promise that they were only the beginning.

They gave him a week to come up with the money, or find some way to get it. They were demanding 10,000 dollars! Some stupid talk about high expenses and interest on the principal. As if he couldn't see it was straight-out robbery, with him cast as the robber!

But his life was worth more than 20,000 dollars, which was a combination of his gambling debt (15,000 by now) and what he had embezzled. And *that* money had to be paid back into the bank's records immediately!

Then, after yet another clash with that blasted kid, and Bess, as usual, taking Donny's side, Linus had the bitter thought: *I wish he'd have an accident — or someone would abduct the little swine* . . .

That was when the magnificent idea had struck him, fully formed, no less!

Arrange a kidnapping, demand a ransom — enough to cover the gambling debt *and* the embezzled money — and all his worries would be over.

The biggest problem would be getting the ransom together. How could he do it? The bank might lend him the money because of his service and position, but there would be close scrutiny of his personal accounts and spending and . . . No, that was out; his embezzlement would soon be discovered.

If he forgot about approaching the bank, that only left Bess and her inheritance. But brother-in-law Carl was the problem there. Tight-fisted, dollar signs where his heart should be.

But, at who knew what cost to his health, he had eventually persuaded Bess to prevail upon Carl to allow her access to the trust fund. After all, Donny was Carl's nephew.

Devlin was agreeable, and that told Linus that the idea must have merit; Devlin was too smart to get involved in anything that could easily go wrong.

He had it all worked out: get the money together, 20,000 dollars, which would allow him to pay off Devlin and put the embezzled money back. Then, write a series of ransom notes, and . . .

But who would pay the money over? Not Linus! Oh, no, he couldn't get involved in that part, but there was Sheriff Cole! A friend, a man handy with a gun in case of unforeseen trouble . . .

That was the answer and, thankfully, Cole had agreed to do the job. A tough man, but still a soft touch in some ways.

But why hadn't it worked? He was certain something must have gone wrong. There should have been word by now, and the boy should have been returned. He should have been notified and . . .

With trembling hand, he reached for the whiskey bottle, surprised to see how little remained. *How many bottles did that make since this horror had started? What did it matter?* He drank it down straight from the neck, jumped when his office door opened and Sheriff Cole strode in, closing the door behind him.

One look at the lawman's face and Linus knew it was all over.

But he had to brazen it out; there was

no other way, and anyway, while he protested his innocence, he might find a solution that would let him off the hook. After all, Cole was a friend, wasn't he, not just a lawman who went blindly by the book . . . ?

And he was a man of honour. Linus had played upon this trait, taken advantage of it, and he would again if he could just find a way to do it.

'What news, Cole?' he rasped, aware that his voice was shaky and that he still held the whiskey bottle by the neck. He gave a fleeting grin, waving the bottle. 'I — I've been worried sick, waiting to hear if everything's all right. It *is* all right, isn't it?'

Cole dropped into the chair opposite the desk, thumbed back his battered hat, hooked a boot over one leg and took out tobacco sack and papers. He began to make a cigarette.

'Donny's home safe with your wife, Linus.'

The banker sighed and his mouth twitched as a laugh of relief wanted to burst out of him. 'Oh, thank God! You don't know how much I appreciate what you've done for me, Cole. And Donny *is* safe and sound? They didn't — harm him?'

Cole shook his head. 'No, he's fine.'

'Good! I admit I don't like the boy very much, but I wouldn't've wished him any real harm.'

'But you took the risk just the same.' Cole cupped a hand around the match flame and glanced across at the banker as he lit the cigarette.

Linus looked grey, sitting stiffly in his chair, frowning now. 'I don't understand. *I* took the risk? What risk are you talking about?'

'You took the risk that Quinlan and the others wouldn't do Donny any real hurt while the ransom was gathered and paid over.'

Linus ran a tongue across dry lips and nodded slowly. 'Well . . . that couldn't be helped. I mean, I don't see how you can think I'm to blame in any way. I had no choice. I was rawhided into finding the ransom money, which I did — as fast as possible. Yes, I suppose, in a way, I *did* take the risk of Donny getting rough treatment, but there was absolutely nothing I could do about it, Cole, you must see that.'

Cole exhaled smoke. 'There would have been no risk at all if you hadn't arranged Donny's kidnapping in the first place, Linus.'

The banker was very still now, eyes almost glazed as he stared unseeingly across his office. It seemed a long time before his gaze focused on Cole's sober face.

'I . . . don't believe I heard you aright, Cole. *I* arranged Donny's kidnapping?' He stood, outraged. 'In the name of God, what're you saying?'

'Sit down, Linus. It's all over now. Almost all over, I guess, is what I mean. It could've worked, but Devlin's men made a mistake. They didn't have a good description of Donny, and identified him by his tow-coloured hair, but mostly by the jacket he was wearing.

Only he'd given it to Sammy Bale after he fell in the river.'

Linus, frowning and trying not to show the trembling that now possessed him, sat down slowly, staring.

'Are you saying . . . do you mean Sammy Bale was abducted istead of Donny?'

'That's it.'

Linus blinked. 'Well, what . . . The ransom . . . They wouldn't've known they had the wrong boy: They'd have believed they had Donny, just taken the ransom and . . . '

His words faded slowly as Cole began to shake his head. Linus slumped.

'Tell me what happened,' he said with sudden resignation.

So Cole told him.

Tears squeezed from Linus Charlton's eyes and rolled down his fat cheeks — no longer pink and healthy looking, but now resembling the gaunt face found on a day-old corpse.

Cole smoked his cigarette down,

thumbed it out in the metal ashtray on the desk.

The banker remained silent, looking down at his finger-locked hands in his lap. Slowly, his haunted eyes lifted to Cole's face and his voice seemed considerably steadier and stronger.

'You killed Quinlan?'

'A bullet was too quick for that son of a bitch, but, yeah, he's dead now. So are some others who worked for Devlin.'

'What about him?'

'I'll ride down and see him. I reckon there're a few charges I can hang on him.'

Linus scoffed. 'Not with the lawyers he'll hire.'

'Then I'll burn down his saloon . . . casino, or whatever he likes to call it.'

'You — you'd do that?'

'Not for you, Linus. But because it's time someone put a stop to Devlin, one way or another.'

'Yes — well, I believe you're probably the only man who could do it, Cole. I suppose Bess knows everything?'

'I didn't tell her.'

Linus smiled ruefully. 'That damn Donny will! Funny thing is, I believe I'm more afraid of Bess than — the bank or even the law.'

'She did say she'd be going to California, and probably staying there.'

The banker almost laughed. 'And just how would she leave me? She's mighty vindictive, Cole. She'll leave my life in utter ruins before she goes, you mark my words. She'll have me humiliated, made a figure of fun and shame . . . '

Cole realized that Linus was probably right and he felt a surge of sympathy for the banker.

'You've been a damn fool, Linus.'

The banker sighed, sat back and spread his hands. He looked at them; the trembling had stopped.

'Yes, I have. And I only have myself to blame.'

Cole stood. 'I won't do you the indignity of putting the manacles on you, Linus, but I want you to come with me. Now.'

'Yes, of course.' He started to open a desk drawer, saying, 'I'll just get a few things and — '

Cole dropped a hand to his gun butt. 'Let's just go, Linus. Get your coat and hat and we'll stroll on down to the law office, just as we've done fifty times in the past. No one needs to know anything's wrong at this stage.'

'Thanks, Cole. You're — considerate.'

The banker went to a closet, put on his grey coat and took down his hat, setting it squarely on his head.

'Do I look my usual smug self?' he asked with a sad smile.

'You look OK.'

Cole held the office door open and Linus pushed past him, pausing to glance around at the clerks working at their desks and behind the counters. He nodded curtly to himself as Cole closed the door.

'One more favour, Cole . . . ?'

'Don't push it, Linus.'

The banker smiled. 'Wouldn't dream of it. Look, I know I have to face Bess. I've got just one shot of whiskey left in my desk bottle. Let me take that one more slug, and then I'll be ready to — to face the music.'

Cole studied his face soberly. Linus met his gaze and smiled faintly.

'For old times' sake, Cole . . . '

A brief hesitation, then the sheriff nodded. 'OK. Don't take too long.'

'No. I won't keep you waiting. Promise.'

He opened the office door and went in quickly, closing the door after him.

Cole leaned his wide shoulders against the office wall, thinking of Bess Charlton and her utter vindictiveness.

What the hell did people, men or women, get out of making life so miserable for so many others? he wondered.

Through the wall, he heard a desk drawer open and, at the same time, remembered seeing the whiskey bottle on Linus's desk.

It had been empty!

He lunged for the door and had it

part-way open when the pistol shot cracked against his ears.

He was just in time to see Linus falling forward across his desk, the small, pearl-handled derringer dropping from his lifeless fingers.

* * *

Cole was behind his own desk, struggling to make out his report for the records, when there was a soft knock on the street door a moment before it opened.

Mattie Bale stepped inside, smiling, still dressed in her dusty clothes from the wild ride into Barberry.

'Am I interrupting?'

'Nothing I can't finish later.' Cole stood up and walked around the desk, offering her the visitor's chair. She smiled as she sat down and he went back around to his own chair. He nodded to the window.

'Getting on for sundown. You'll be driving in the dark.'

'I've decided to stay over in town tonight. Sammy will enjoy it. He's playing with Donny Charlton at the livery just now. Well, not playing, more like working. Earl's promised them two bits each if they fork some hay for him. I suspect they'll only be moving it from one place to another. But he likes kids, does Earl.'

'Yeah — a real family man.'

'Forgive me if I'm prying, Sheriff, but you seem to me like you'd make a good . . . family man.'

He met her steady gaze. 'Once, maybe.' Then without conscious volition, he added, 'There was a fire. My wife and son — didn't get out in time.'

She reached across the desk and her small hand squeezed his — a spontaneous gesture of sympathy.

'I'm sorry if I stirred . . . bad memories.'

He smiled. 'No bad memories. I just think about the good times, and the good times that might've been.'

She nodded slowly. 'Well, that's a fine

way to handle such a tragedy.'

'I've only just managed to figure it out. For a long time there I — I lived too much in the past.'

'I'm glad things are better for you now, then. I want to thank you for saving Sam. It was very brave.'

'Wish I'd got there sooner.'

'I'm very grateful. What'll happen to Winston?'

'He's in the cells with another man named Creed. They'll both be facing the judge in a few days.'

She nodded a little absently, tapping work-worn fingers against the edge of his desk. 'I didn't really come to ask about Winston,' she confessed and his smile grew wider. 'Oh! You knew! I must be more transparent than I thought.'

'Well, I figure you for a good woman, Mattie, but I don't see you as worrying too much about Winston's welfare.'

She laughed briefly. 'No. He deserves some time in jail. What I really came for was to ask you . . . if you're ever out our way, near the farm, that is, why don't you stop by and I'll cook you a meal? I mean, being a bachelor, you must grow tired of buying indifferent food and — '

'Sure. That's a good idea. I'll be coming by to get your statement in a day or so . . . '

'I could give it to you now. Oh! Yes, yes do that, Cole. Try to make it about lunchtime.'

He stood and reached down his hat from the wall peg. 'All this talk about food's making me hungry. How about I buy you supper at Farrel's diner? They do a good pot-roast on a Thursday night . . . '

'This is Friday.'

'They serve it cold on Fridays, with a fresh salad. Mighty good on the palate, so they say. Sometimes even have ice cream for later.'

She laughed and took the arm he offered her as they made for the office door.

'I think we'd better check it out, don't you?'

'Best idea I've heard today. C'mon.'